THE NEW-CLASSIC SCIENCE FICTION
SERIES
of
SHORT STORIES FROM THE LIGHTER
SIDE

BOOK TWO

Orbital Spam

TREVOR WATTS

Dedicated to Chris Watts
For her editing skills, commitment and tolerance.

Log on to https://www.sci-fi-author.com/
Facebook at Creative Imagination

First Printing: September 2020
Brinsley Publishing Services

ISBN: 9798657438079

Table of Contents

APACE

'You are charged. Therefore you are guilty. There is no plea.'

The Lord High Provost affirmed it, 'This Martial Court is held for the official record: that the background be clarified; the charge be formalised; and sentence be passed.'

The prisoner sighed, gazed at the three Judges Ultima, and consulted his Aide, 'I wish to speak.'

'Shortly. You are Commander Herak Lees, born on Alcmene, largest moon of the planet Ze'us?

'I am.'

'You understand the charge? You defied direct orders to engage the enemy – to "Attack Apace". Your delay of three days resulted in the deaths of approximately four thousand eight hundred civilians on the colony planet Pasithia?'

Herak Lees nodded and stared at the three Lords Provost, Council and Civil seated above. This was all a show for the array of recorders and witnesses. In a few minutes he would be executed by electro-bolt. It was always the way when matters got this far – a brilliant flesh; an acrid tinge to the nostrils; a slight swirl of smoke; and an empty dock where the prisoner had been standing. Not something he habitually watched, but there had been a lot of replays and simulations in recent days.

Swallowing hard, and hoping he didn't disgrace himself, his unit and his family, Lees stood as firmly as he was able.

Very well,' Civil Lord Urbana took over. 'To summarise: Pasithia is Planet 13, and the most recent one that we have begun to colonise. As such it has a population of only five hundred thousand, each one of whom is a vital part of the fledgling economy. Thus, when there was an attack by a triple force of Lewishian SN ships, our people were totally unprepared and extremely vulnerable. Initial slaughter was massive, until the population managed to organise some kind of defence, and to contact Federation Central.

'Central, naturally, despatched a counter force that was capable of repelling the invasion. Yours, Commander. "Attack *Apace*, Repel and Destroy" was the order, was it not?'

Lees nodded.

'Answer!' Lord Provost demanded.

'Yes, it was.'

'Do you not understand "Apace"?'

'It means as fast as possible,' Commander Lees obliged, allowing the inevitable to take its course. The arc electrodes were embedded in the ceiling above and the floor beneath his feet.

'Before the sentence is formalised and carried out…' Lees knew there was only one verdict and one sentence – Being charged came hand-in-hand with the guilty verdict. 'Now. In accordance with your rights, is there anything you wish say or ask?'

'Yes. Why was Pasithia completely unprotected when it is so isolated and vulnerable?'

'This is not a forum to discuss such matters. Anything else?' The Lord Provost reached for *The Red Button.*

'Yes. Why was I chosen? I wasn't the closest force, was I? In fact, three other Federal forces were considerably closer?'

'Er… This is not the place to discuss such things.'

'Was it thought that I and my force were the most experienced, or prepared, of our available forces?'

'Indeed, yes.' The Lord Council, decked in all his finery, looked relieved that he could agree with something, for the sake of the record.

'In what way? Years of service? Successes in my record?'

'Yes – both.' Something else he could agree with. 'You are by far the most experienced and successful— Er… Yes. And…' His note of triumph was evident, 'You were already out and active.'

'Was any other force available?'

'Er… this is most irregular. No, three defence forces are temporarily de-commissioned; two have retired; two are undergoing refits.'

'So, I was judged to be the most experienced commander you had available; the most successful in terms of my record; and already in full prepared mode?'

'Yes. And thus you should have followed orders, and attacked apace.' Council permitted himself a smug gaze around the assembly.

'But you are untruthing, aren't you?' Lees persisted. *At least I'll make it uncomfortable for them… inform the public of the real situation.* 'Omitting? Slanting your implications? If you had carried out standard monitoring of all forces, you must have known that we were *not* in fully-prepared mode, but were deeply engaged in conflict with the Konya uprising forces. You would surely not have had only one single Defence Force to call on – for the whole of our Protectorate? And deployed it towards the far fringe of Federal Territory, with no other cover.'

'It there a relevant question here?' The Lord Provost's finger twitched towards the final button again.

'My Lord Provost and his Admiral Officers were fully aware of this situation, and chose to ignore it, leaving all Federation planets wide open—'

'This line of questioning must cease. Operational matters are not on trial here. You are.'

'Just so. My Over-command Officer, Admiral Lord Kellick, was fully aware of my situation in the Konya Quadrant. He was paying a Watch Visit when the order came through. As I said, I was not in FP Mode: my force was still actively and heavily engaged with large contingents of well-armed rebel groups that were well dug in on a broad front of asteroids, moons and rocklets. I pointed out that we would be wiped out if we attempted to withdraw instantly. To extract safely from those engagements would take at least one day. Our departure would also result in the rebels taking control of the whole Konya System.

'Admiral Lord Kellick was fully aware of this and ordered me to disengage my force *with all due safety*. Which we did, taking one full day. He then required to be taken to Federation Central, rather than accompany the force to Pasithia. That was one day out of our direct route. He also sanctioned the Enforced Rest Period between major engagement – The compulsory One Day in Deep Sleep for all combatants, to rebuild their minds. Is he not available as my witness?'

'He is not.'

Lees paused for breath, taking the time to stare into the uncompromising face of each judge in turn, and to glance at the ceiling panels that hid the electrodes. 'Further, we were in Actual Engagement Mode, not Full Prepared, as you must know.'

'Er... The difference being?' The Lord Civil displayed his ignorance of military matters.

'Fully Prepared is defined as "A complete complement of informed, trained and rested personnel, with equipment and craft in full working condition."

'Did your Lordships have any awareness of my force's condition? We were eighteen key officers lost; one hundred and eighteen troopers; one third of our equipment damaged, lost or otherwise "unavailable for use", as regulations have it. And two-thirds of our power and ammunition was expended. In fact, we were fending off the attacks on our positions whilst awaiting long-overdue replacements, were we not?'

The three Lords Provost, Council and Civil glanced between themselves, muttering, 'This is irrelevant. Sentence is—'

'No it isn't.' Commander Lees' Brevet Aide-à-Court spoke for the first time. 'Verdict must be formalised before sentence is stated or carried out. And it cannot be formalised until the Accused has ended his statement.'

She paused, mostly to control her nerves. 'According to the official inventory,' Brevet Aide-à-Court Marta Karys consulted the screen by her side, 'Two hundred

Personnel had been placed in Cryo not long before this crisis arose; but no-one had thought to begin the two-day revival programme to make them available, had they?

'It was,' she continued, '*impossible* for Commander Herak to attack *apace* – he did not have the capability to launch any meaningful attack; he lacked the power to travel right across the Federal Territory in under two days; his whole force needed replenishment in numbers and strength. He was, in fact, given an order that was impossible to obey under the circumstances.'

The Lordly Threesome barely hesitated, 'Verdict is confirmed. Sentence is—'

'So! My Lords, you are happy to execute the *only* experienced Force Commander in the Federal Navy? The *only* one with any real experience – since all others are newly-appointed, retired or have been "decommissioned"? You must be aware that the Federation has already lost control of the Konya System since Commander Herak Lees was withdrawn? And that Parthan and Jayaster arc being encroached upon by unfriendly forces? And also,' she paused for breath while she had their full attention, 'that the hard-defended Pasithia – rescued and saved by Commander Lees – has since come under renewed attack by the Lewishians at a cost of over two thousand persons per day?'

'These are operational matters. Not for open discussion here.'

The ceiling panels slid aside. 'There is self-evident guilt in this instance.'

'The verdict is confirmed. Sentence will—' All three Lords were reaching for *The Red Button*, 'be carried out at once.'

'Halt the proceeding.'

Eyes had no idea which way to turn. The voice had come from all around.

'Sentence will be carried out in accordance with the Will of the People.'

The triple flash was eye-searing in its brilliance, made worse by the stinging smoke of vaporised flesh, bone and uniform as the Lords Provost, Council and Civil disintegrated.

Swallowing hard, expecting to be next on the list, Brevet Aide-à-Court Marta Karys and Commander Lees braced themselves.

'Lord High Provost Herak Lees, take up your post apace and defend The Federation.' The disembodied voice finished, 'By decree of the Accumulated Wisdom of the People.'

'Accum..? Huh?' Stunned and shaking, Herak Lees weakly looked about him.

'All the recorders,' his Aide waved vaguely around, 'the witnesses. In major cases of Federation-wide importance, they allow for cumulative verdicts to be made – the people vote by proxaria. The voice is that of "The People". I've never heard it before. It should be on the screen soon... Ahh... here... Almost fifty percent of the Federation population have watched, and voted – around eleven billion persons. Ninety-two percent voted in favour of a redirection of the charge.'

She offered the faintest and most fleeting of smiles, 'We'd better get a move on, Commander Herak Lees: Your order was to Defend the Federation *Apace*. And my bladder is calling me fairly desperately.'

COME AGAIN?

'Face it, Bari,' I said, 'we're washed-up on Kalèdas, the most backvac planet in the galaxy. A full summer and autumn in the orchards, fields, forest…' I waved a couple of sensicles round the hostel where three dozen of us gutter-workers had been dossing down during the grubbing season. 'We'll have to move on soon.'

'At least we've been herding the koyun sheep, not slopping the piggers out.' Bari nodded, chewing on a sweet-stick from the discards heap.

'That's because we learned the mecho-side of things in the Corps.' Pasti laughed in his own little way – all shivering tendrils and quivery frills. 'At least we came out the fighting with some skills, eh?'

This whole region was sure nothing to shout about, much less fight over. But The Federation laid claim to it, and The Empire wanted it. Nobody knew who won in the end; the fighting seemed to peter out when the wounded weren't being treated any longer, no replacements, no supplies, no ammo, and nobody came to evacuate us remnants. Dumped, we were, in a cess-pit like Kalèdas.

'You know,' I decided, 'I'm gonna try and get home myself. Stuff the Fed; we'll be in the poverty queues if we stay here with no work.'

'Home?' Pasti piped up. 'Which planet are you from, Voskós? None of us is wanted back home, wherever we come from.'

9

'Well, we're not welcome round here, that's for sure, post-season.' Bari tottered closer, tall but limping on only five legs – something broken in the other one. Pasti, as always, stayed close by his side. He had to; he didn't see much, not with milky, radiated eyes perched up on stalks.

'Me,' I said, 'I've had enough. I'm going down the Eastside space port at Rigel. They're not fussed about IDs at the freight depot, with all the itinerants sleeping in the dorms – looking for a berth or a stowaway chance.'

'Where'd we go?'

'Right now, it's home I prefer.'

They shook and humffed and I-dunno-ed; and thought of reasons why none of their home planets was all that appealing nowadays, but the three-fold consensus was that we had nothing to lose by trying to leave Kalèdas.

* * *

So we upped ourselves, and wriggled it down to the Rigel Depot. Only took a half-day. The whole depot was in chaos – crowded; all jostling and shuffling.

'Some craft's arrived unexpectedly, and parked up in orbit,' a Yuke at the back desk told us. 'Shuttle take-offs are cancelled; nothing's moving; no connections for anywhere.' He smiled like Yukes always do – with both faces, and mandibles a-quiver.

'Unexpected arrival?' I said. 'Hardly a rarity.'

'Yeah, but this one just turned-up outa nowhere, ten times the size of anything else. Called the Door Ka Taara.'

Some other official joined in, local guy – looking ridiculous with them over-painted eye-stalks that's all

10

the fashion this season. 'It's real Outworld linguistics they got – struggling to communicate. Seems they ain't lost exactly – more like they lost something and ain't shifting till they found it.'

'So we aren't going anywhere?' I summed it up.

'Nobody is – huge backlog of flights. Look round – Yukes and Yumes galore; Ales; Crits – like you two.' He nodded to Bari and Pasti.

'There's even a couple of Wingies – silverhead queenies,' his colleague said. 'We've never seen them here before. It's rumoured they're off the Faraway Star – the Door Ka Taara.'

'Nobody's got accommodation. See outside? Two dozen shuttles waiting. Security's high, so a few quiddles to the Load Chief won't get you aboard any of'em.'

So we wrigged-it round to the passenger terminal. It was heaving even more. Didn't seem worth milling round with the rest, so we decided, 'It's getting late; nowhere to head-down, so shall we grab a bite, and try the Shelter?'

'*The Shelter?* Really?' It's ten floors underground through solid concrete and steel.'

'It's damp, cold…'

'Filthy…'

'Look around – we ain't gonna find a head-spot here.'

'It's maybe got room…' Bari wavered.

'I suppose we might as well.' Pasti gave in.

***

It took a bit of finding: the old beacon and siren were gone – collapsed a yonk back. So outsiders don't know

11

about it. And it sure don't look much, under concrete roofing, and blast-baffle entrances.

It was just as bad down there, umpteen steps buried in litter and debris; couple of drunk skit-bugs mumbling the night away in the dimness... Yumes and Crits wandering along dim corridors.

'Yeah,' Bari said, once we got down to the lowest level, 'The Pit Floor. Smell the sewage? Should be a gateman somewhere, keeping tabs.'

'Keeping tabs? How? It's filthy, cold...'

'He sluices the drains, burns the litter, shifts the bodies, knows where there's a space for newcomers, collects payments and— Hey! This'll be him.'

Trundling in our direction was a pseudo, the wonky head sort. 'Gents?' At least he was half-curled antennae from the off – always a good sign with pseudos.

'Got any room?' Pasti asked. Gateman shook his flanges – Pasti shook his back in hope. 'So you have?'

'Nope.'

I reached out, all mental and tenty, as they say – I can be really pathetic-looking when I put that tinge of purple into my tentacle tips.

'You'll be breaking my oil-seals, Gentlemen,' Gateman chuntered. 'I got no rooms, no beds... can't feed you. Don't matter what you offer.'

'Wasn't offering anything.' Pasti did his best to get us thrown out.

'Oh, I kinda hoped you maybe would.' He wilted a fraction.

'What you after? A battery-charge?' Bari laughed in that weird way Crits do.

'For a couple of copper-disks I can maybe find something shared for you.'

'Can we take a look?'

'What? You're getting fussy? We'll take it,' I decided for us.

'Third turning left,' he squeaked after us as we traipsed towards the bleak-lit corridors. 'End room. There's a light on.'

They were all store rooms, service and utility spaces... cold and damp. Dim nightlights at best. 'What you got us into, Voskós?'

'Stop moaning. It's better'n being on the surface on a night like this.'

'Third left? This one?'

'Yeah, there's a light at the end...'

So we trudged down – Bari limping worse after so much moving upright. End room. A light glowed through the panel above the door. 'Somebody's brought their own light,' Pasti chuntered. 'I'll never sleep with that on.'

'He said shared. Don't want no trouble, Bari, whatever they are.'

'Me? Trouble?'

I knocked, sort of polite, and went in, the others utching me into the warmth.

'Stuffitall; it's a machinery room.' Pasti's never happy for long.

A huge iron pump-wheel dominated, all rusted and stark in that light. Heaps of crates along the wall, bales of textiles, storage shelves. Must have been twenty skitterlings squatting round on the floor but could hardly see them in the shadows – the light radiated from the far side of a stack of bed-frames and table-tops, so it was mostly the concrete ceiling that was illuminated, not them.

'Let's go see what's making the light, huh?' Tripping over a few skitterlings; them and their whispering little voices.

I looked round the stack. The light was coming from a Wingie! Wow... I'm thinking. A Wingie. Down here in this cellar-pit. Wasn't no silverhead Queenie, either. 'It's an *anjelios* Wingie, a Golden King.'

I'd never seen one before. It was awesome: gossamer-gold wings outspread, like on the vids. It was croodled over something, its wings slowly spreading out and closing again, like a huge protecting umbrella. All gleaming gold and sheeny, bathed in its own light.

I was just struck, staring. Couldn't breathe. I think Pasti and Bari were the same. It was a spares-crate he was hovering over... X4 pump valves, it said on the side. The light was coming out the crate.

I took a very trembly step forward. Another, trying to see what's got the anjelios' attention in there, buried in wrapping rags.

Something moved. Two miniscule, slender fingers reached up out the bundle of rags. That stopped me dead. They kinda grasped at nothing, flexing… seeking around. A tiny face rose, gazed around; sort of all-knowing. I took a couple more steps forward, like I needed to see… be near it. But I was sinking… on my knees. Bari and Pasti came close, too, and sank down next to me.

'Kutsal İsa!' Pasti muttered, absolutely awed.

'Bu Isa.' Bari could scarcely get the words between his mandibles.

'This's the Kurtarici – *The Saviour.'* I could hardly breathe for just looking at it.

'It's the baby that ship's come looking for, the Door Ka Taara… The Faraway Star.'

I reached. Its eyes lit on me and smiled. Tiny fingers grasped so softly round my sucker tip. I'd gone all warm inside. *'Saviour,'* I said.

I knew I'd never be the same again.

FIRST CALL, LAST CALL

'Sub? Those signals we picked up two deccas ago?'

'Hmm?' Loxey was hunched over the set we'd cobbled together and finally created enough background power to pick up general comms traffic.

'I've just been receiving again, lasted three minutes. Five channels together, I think, faint, and jumbled across each other on close-parallel bands.'

'Same as last decc? What's your interpretation?'

'Don't want to get your hopes up—'

'Loxey! Just tell me! Sorry – didn't mean to— Just say it.'

'Fragments point to the war coming to an end. In our favour. Alliance forces have broken through – can't make out where – and the Perfids are in general retreat. That's just the notion I get, what the mass of it sounds like. No guarantees on it.'

'Really?' *After five years' war? Three since the Hospital Ship First Call, was crippled and taken in a raid attack.* There we'd been, all red-crossed and broadcasting wide and loud on the medi-beacons. We're unarmed, in a recognised neutral orbit, and they fire on us, with no warning. Incapable of offering resistance. What with? Bone patches and burns bindings? Two neutron bolts took our motors out.

'Sub. It's not definite. It's just how it sounds on half a dozen intermixed signal-bursts.'

'I get that. I listened to the first ones, didn't I?'

The Perfid ship had no bother grappling us – with no engines, and down to battery power – and piggy-backed the First Call completely out of that system, into orbit off some other planet that we think must be Perfida, their home planet. We're mere trophies, of no worth, and they don't speak with such sub-beings. So here we've been parked, for three thousand two hundred orbits of this planet, without any provision of power, food or drink for three years. We were extremely fortunate not to have had full casualty bays when we were taken, but we've been moderately desperate of late. Deaths are 58% of original complement of officers, crew and passenger-patients. That varies – 100% among officers – the Perfids didn't like officers attempting to negotiate better conditions, so they routinely slaughtered anyone who made any "demands", or was in any kind of decorated clothing.

'No details on any ships? Planets? Commodore names? Force codes? Casualties?'

'All snatches. Nothing coherent. A lot of it is impressions, odd words and phrases.'

'You've told no-one else?'

'You said not to.'

Sure I did, and I'm in command, aren't I? Huh. I'm a self-appointed Brevet Subaltern. I was Second Crewman in the maintenance unit – hardly officer grade. So, being the only Seconder left – all the others dead, disappeared or resigned – I promoted myself to Subaltern. That's the highest grade a crew member can become, and the lowest level for a starter-officer. The Brevet bit means I don't get paid; it's merely a title, making me a target for Perfid malice.

They come to me for things – usually demands for information, as if any of us knows anything. I always whinge that we have no resources, and are desperate for medical supplies, water, power for heating… I show them how limited we are, and offer the records to prove it. They took exception last time I did that, when they wanted medical supplies that they'd confiscated from us two years previously. Atrax lost his temper and sliced the two stores personnel in half. Peet Buzzy and Jane the Main. For me, that was the worst: Jane and I had a thing, we were marrying and settling on Taivas when this was all over.

I about gave up after that; I so wanted to die. I railed at them as I cleaned up two bodies, in four pieces, and a flood of blood. More so these days – I push them. I want to be out of this utter hell. They know what state we're in, and that I'm suicidal over it all by now. So they keep me alive to spite me.

When I get started on them, their arm-legs start quivering – the front half-dozen, anyway. We think that's laughing; they're entertained by my fury and begging. Sometimes, their front four eyes vibrate in and out as well, probably a sign of anger. Plus, when they've killed one of us, their upper head mass, which is a peacock pattern anyway, brightens and fades in a rhythm. They're weird, more like spiders than the arapanids they're classed as. They certainly have no humanity in them – the whole thought of empathy seems to be beyond them. They just don't understand fellow-feeling; don't care.

We all want out of this. We've considered self-detonating the ship, but we can't get the power high enough. Ideally, we want to take one of their ships with us.

On top of their whimsical killing, general starvation and cold, there's radiation seeping through the shielding

– some passengers and crew are getting really sick now, especially with the stench since the recycling packed up. Life is just death around here.

No medical or other supplies come through. They won't permit any contact from home. It's totally against Agreed Interstellar Law. We know the Alliance will have protested about attacking a Hospital Ship, made representations for our release, and sent frequent consignments and mail, but it's all ignored or intercepted. No news of families, communications blocked, our supplies stolen or destroyed. Probably merely for their amusement.

The last three senior officers who demanded, complained and suggested, in that order, found out about lack of compassion the hardest way. We've not seen or heard from them after they were forcibly escorted off-ship. Other crew and patient-passengers disappeared; some were experimented on – a few came back without eyes, tongues, genitals, arms… There are arbitrary punishments for even looking in their direction on the odd occasion they come aboard. The stars alone know why they come – just to stir up some fun, it seems; they're in a permanently bad mood.

My last suicide bid, two deccs ago, was a rant at Atrax and two of his regular cronies about providing us with food and home contact. It wasn't entirely suicide-oriented – I needed to divert their attention from the receiver apparatus we had set up in the command room, with just enough power to pick up the faintest and briefest zips from Common Base. And we were just receiving our first general communications when the bloody Perfid ship thunked into us and they were swarming all over us like they knew something was amiss. They always think something's amiss, and usually kill whoever happens to be in their way.

That little fracas cost me half my face. I look an absolute Mangle-heap now. Feel like it, too.

Not that I can feel too much – one of them burned my left-hand fingers off about a year ago. They thought that was a hoot, too. They made hooting sounds, anyway, along with all eight eyes going into glittery extra time.

'You truly believe the Alliance is winning, Lox?'

'Not just winning, Sub. It really sounds like the major breakthrough. These latest transmissions very much indicate our forces are sweeping through their defences on at least three fronts.'

'If the rad pickups are genuine. It couldn't be the Perfids amusing themselves?'

'It's not the way they're acting. I'm sure they're unaware of this equipment. Gheas and Gilly reckon they were especially edgy on their flying visit yesterday.'

'If the Humanic Alliance gets this far, there could be unfortunate repercussions for us. They'll kill us all; get rid of the evidence. They know they're breaking the Covenants of War, and are probably counting on us not realising. They'll be afraid we might organise resistance in the hope of delaying them long enough for our people to arrive.'

A party came forcing in, same as always. No warning. They did it one time and the airlock wasn't sealed. We lost seven personnel to the vac, and they rampaged through whichever part of the ship took their hairypincered fancy. We keep the inner airlock sealed all the time since then.

In they came, yesterday, all weaponed-up, same as always. Head patterns vivid as sunrise on Majesta.

I met them, as the only thing that resembles an officer – i.e., more ripped apart than most – did I mention the leg I lost to a stray bolt last year? I had two other crew with me – it was their turn on the front line. With the Perfids' usual charm, I was pinned to the wall with claws in my throat – they forget that I can't answer like that. Two years ago, they ripped the Sub-Cap's head off when he couldn't answer – that was another occasion when there was blood all over the plating. A pair of them were sucking it up as they dragged him out.

Leading the Perfid squad this time, it was Atrax, the High Kaz of their prison contingent. He's the chief scum, sadist and couldn't-care-lesser. With cronies – I recognised Ctenus and Laziod. If they have females, I think that's what these two are. Two dozen more came skittering in behind them, pulling large blue-irrid cases. *They're explosive charges. They're not taking chances on us. So it's all true, then? They're losing?*

I was laughing – as much as I might with a pair of pincers round my throat. Plus half my mouth, cheek and one eye gone. Atrax realised something – his eyes have this way of shining in rotation, all the way round. His pincers relaxed and he chittered in bastardised Stang-cum-Perfy, 'You are amused.'

'You wait till now to give us what we want? To kill us all?' I speak the worked-out language better than he does, and spat into his oesophageal opening. 'Come on, coward. Finish me. Lose your poisonous little temper, you foul hairbag.' Okay, he wouldn't get some of the words, but he understood, alright. His pincers clenched in. *Come on. You bastard arapanid bag of shit,'* I choked. 'Come on, do it.'

He eased off again. A point was forming below his e-opening, swelling out. That's his venom gland, usually tucked behind a double flap; I once saw him use it on a bone-setter doctor; for no apparent reason. *Shit – he's going to paralyse me. But I'll be immune to pain when it all goes up.*

'You want me to.' His eyes glitter-fixed on me, ominously colour-changing.

'Oh yes, Atrax. Do it. There'll be pieces in orbit for years. We know you're losing. The Humanic Alliance will be here soon, won't they? They'll know.'

He was in pause mode. Venom gland poised. 'You will never be found. You will be dead in a million shreds.' He even *felt* cold then.

'The Perfida are beaten, Atrax. The Alliance has the technology to discover what happened to us, then you'll all be dead, too, and your planet down there. Think we don't know where we are? Perfida is a beautiful planet, isn't it? Peaceful, untouched by the war, stuffed with your treasures? Oh, no – you don't do beauty, do you? Not other people's, anyway.'

You're not understanding this, are you? Beetle?

'You are nothing. Inferior.'

'So stop wasting your time. End me. End the ship. And yourselves. End your planet. Go on. *Coward.'* *Shuggerit! His eyes are lighting up like a kaleido-rotor. He's furious, barking something at the others. They're still arranging the cases, wiring them together; fixing wi-o units.*

His grip re-tightened. 'Tell me your meaning.'

'Alliance ships will come. They will identify scraps of the Hospital Ship First Call that vanished three years ago; and will know that you kept us here, starving, for three years. What do you think they will do then?'

'You are amused.'

'Shuggs, yes. I would love to watch your home planet disintegrate – it takes around two days for the molecular disruptors to start the chain reaction. Then your planet will slowly eat itself. To ruin. So, yes. I am amused.'

He understood *all* of that. 'How you know?' He chirruped.

'Know what? That's it's Perfida down there? Or that the Commonwealth is a few days away? Or how the disruptor engines work? I'm an engineer, maintenance. I fixed the rads, the batteries, the viewers. I worked on disruptors at Soltau Base, years ago. They've only been used twice – one a test, the other against Thoris. They're aching to use one for real. And you? Perhaps you'll be half dismembered, watching your home planet dying.'

He let me go. Backed off. Barked to the others. They ceased their busying with the heap of cases.

Ah. You're thinking in overdrive. So it's true then, we are winning. Our ships will be here soon –ish. And you're imagining your sacred home planet becoming a heap of wind-blown dust. Good. You can suffer for a change.

'Come on, Atrax. Do it. I don't care. You'll be signing the Death Note for your whole existence – all your species. Destroying a hospital ship? Dismembering is the least of what they'll do to you. Maybe the slow disruptors? A single one? Absolutely unstoppable once started. Takes so much longer to eat a planet.'

Yes, your colour-patterning keeps fading, then going vivid again; neck hairs erect. You're upset, eh? First time ever, you arrogant arapanid. It was quite a warming experience for me. 'You'll all watch the disintegration eating towards you, and blaming *you.*' *For two dozen joyful, delicious days of utter panic.*

'So just put us out of this hell… and yourselves into your own abyss.'

He waved and hooted back to his underlings. They backed away. 'You tell no truth.'

'What have I got to lose? You think life's worth living without your pincers? sensicles? If half your eyes were torn out? You'd live like I do, eh?'

I imagine he was thinking furiously. It went on for long minins. 'Subaltern – You think you have an alternative. To save yourselves.'

Did I? A thought was growing.

'The Alliance ships will soon be here. Will you fight? Make them angry so they you? Then they'll discover a cloud of small pieces of our wreckage, perhaps on a trajectory into your sun? They will be even more angry that you have not only illegally captured a helpless hospital ship; and tortured all the humans aboard. But you then destroy it to cover your sin. So what will their anger be vented on? Your vicious little planet down there, perhaps?'

'We will spare you.'

'Three years too late, Atrax, High Kaziri. Alive or dead, they will see, and wipe out creatures that consider it normal to do this.' *Come on, think of it, you stupid Perf. Do I have to under-fyking-line it?* 'However,' *He's giving me the glittery eyes treatment.* 'If you had already ceased to fight, and had no weapons…' *Come on… realise…*

'If we had no weapons…? Ah… yes, I see what you're thinking. That we would change roles. You would hold the weapons.'

At last, you hairy spidrous creature, keep going…

'We would appear to be the prisoners of you.'

Come on, you vicious coward. Can't think the unthinkable? Do I have to do all the prompting? 'Our people honour their prisoners,' I told him, quite loftily. 'If you were already our prisoners, they would do nothing to harm you.'

'Or Perfida.' Loxey backed me up.

'Your planet would be safe, if it was considered to be no longer at war.' Gheas had cottoned-on, too.

It took Atrax a long time to think it through; to talk with his party; to scrabble off-ship and confer with all the rest of the sadistic arapanid creatures who were above him – he was little more than liaison officer cum prison guard – High Kaz.

He returned several hours later, with a party of Perfs who were new to me. Dressed – like Atrax – in "uniforms", with extra sashes and insignia. For such apparently high-up ones to visit a pack of captured unworthies was unprecedented.

'It has been decided,' my still-arrogant High Kaz said, 'that you will be presented with a token weapon. It will appear that we are under your care.'

So, for all your hooting and whirring, you've still not fully seen the light for your own survival? And that of your diamantic little planet down there, hmm?

26

'I think they'd notice if we only had a single "token".'

Atrax and Co did a bit of arm-foot twiddling and proboscal twisting, conferring. And wanted to know my view.

You really can't put yourself into someone else's point of view, can you? You're ripe for this. 'The Alliance Delegation would see that we are still your captives.' *Yes, you're understanding that. You just need a bit more push.* 'The crew of the First Call need to be in possession of the only weapons that are up here, in orbit, so it would be clear.'

'We do not surrender.'

'It's up to you, how you see it. You own us. We are totally at your non-existent mercy. I merely say that they would see the sham of any mere token.'

They're thinking about it, coming to see the writing on the bulkhead. 'You think we should give you more?'

'Perhaps so, High Kaziri. We could hardly use them against you if you had vacated the First Call, and left us here alone with a few weapons, could we? Whatever you think.'

With considerable argumentative hootling and whirriting, they placed a selection of weapons in the centre of the airlock reception space. 'You could leave the explosives – show what you could have done, were you not so merciful.' They don't really understand "merciful" but they left the blue cases, and I waved a stumpy hand after them when they eventually departed with their two-dozen bright-patterned troops. *Craven creatures; I hate you.*

They're now saying it's a day at most till the first Humanic ship arrives. They're preparing "an honourable welcome".

Yes, I do have a plan. I feel quite – not smug, more *settled* – about it. It would be nice to watch it come into fruition, but, if I plan it well, I know it will work. First, after three years of brutality and deceit against us, I'm counting on my crew and passengers not fully trusting the Perfids – they still refer to it as a cessation, or truce, not a surrender. And with the Alliance's years of experience in dealing with them, fighting against them, I expect the first humanic delegation will be particularly circumspect in their approach and subsequent dealings – they'll be prepared for any trouble the Perfids attempt to cause. Any treachery will be met with immediate retaliation.

So I must ensure that the Perfids do perpetrate some terrible, bad-faith deed against the ship that comes to accept their surrender.

'Gentlemen, Lady,' I addressed Loxey, Gheas and Gilly in the airlock reception area. Their understanding had to be what I decided, regardless of any reality; or second-guessing what the Perfids actually intended to do. 'I need everyone except me to be as far from this area as possible – get into the storage compartments on G Deck 4; lock them up, seal them, stay there.'

'But everyone wants to be here for the arrival… welcome the troops, the delegation.'

'They *need* to be here, Sub.'

'We're saved.'

'Not yet, we aren't. You trust the Perfids? You think they'll allow us to regale our rescuers with three-years' worth of horror stories. If we all gathered here, what do you imagine they'd be tempted to do? See the explosives they've left all around?'

Surely not—'

'Surely yes. They've re-rigged them. I watched, thought they were disconnecting them, but they've merely re-wired and re-aligned them – much of the blast going outwards—'

'Into any Alliance ship that was docked against us?'

'Bastards!'

'Typical.'

Oh, good. You cotton on quick. 'You all need to be safely away from this area. On G Deck.'

'What are you going to do? Stay here? Attempt to stop them? Warn the Alliance ship?'

Come on, be convincing, they have to believe this. 'Yes, I'll try. I know how they've done the re-wiring. Maybe I can disconnect at least some of them, or possibly set it off early to warn the Alliance ship before it links alongside. It'll just destroy this immediate area if I can do that.'

'But you'll…'

Yes… Loxey believes that it's what they'd do… and Gilly always trusts what I say, especially anything against the Perfies. They'll be perfect witnesses that we believe our captors are still in their murderous spidery mentality. Even Gheas will admit that I was right, for once.

'You'd better go now. They're expecting the vanguard Alliance vessel to be here in a day or two. You'll be okay. G Deck is self-sustaining; you'll survive any explosion up here, and the rescue. Reset the emergency beacons – they're powered up. Set them broadcasting now, so the Alliance squads'll know you're still aboard and alive.'

The Perfids appear to believe they're still in control, and that this will merely be a transfer of captured property.

I've been alone in the upper decks for almost two days; plenty long enough to defuse most of the blue cases, and fit my own wi-o units to a set of them. The Humanic Alliance WS Mighty is manoeuvring closer, and the Perfid greeting party has joined me in HS First Call's reception bay. They seem to think there's something to discuss, to negotiate; they still haven't come to terms with the concept of surrender, not when it comes to the glorious bastion of their own home planet.

But the people aboard the War Ship Mighty must know what they're like, and be ready to respond in a variety of appropriate ways. They'll have something to respond to in just a moment, when I trigger the detonators. The whole Reception area will erupt, with the main directional blast aimed through the airlock, where – if the Mighty was alongside – it would cripple them, and wipe out their boarding party.

But it'll go off early. The Mighty will survive intact, but furious at this typical Perfid betrayal – an attempt to harm the Alliance ship, and destroy the evidence of the HS First Call's years of pitiless imprisonment.

The rest of the crew will vouch that we suspected the Perfids would try something like this, and that I had remained here, hoping to thwart any such attempt.

The Alliance will promptly take their revenge on the species that would do this – living down there in utter luxury, plundering planets and despising all. It'll be a wind-swept wasteland before the decc is out.

Now then... Yessss.... the War Ship Mighty is at just about the perfect distance for a nasty, and very irritating, scorch...

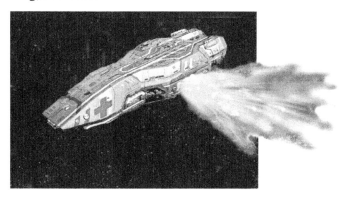

I CAN ONLY TAKE SO MUCH

'I can only take so much. Those awful insects insist on crawling into my clothes, Millions of them. All biting and nipping and stinging. Look at my face. I was covered in them. Could hardly see anything. They must have pumped a gallon of their stinging poisonous gunge into me. I expect I have haemo-venom or something, instead of blood.'

'They're not in your clothes now, Miss Madeleine.' I loved Natalia's hands on me. So delicious; her skin so golden; her touch so light. As light as my well-practised fingers traced their delicate trails over her so-fine curves. 'They might be. It's me that's not in my clothes.'

Natalia, my room maid, my bed friend, my soul-mate for the week at the lodge, said they were *insectos tigre* in Spanish, and something utterly unpronounceable in the local Indian language. 'Tiger insects. They never being eaten by bats. We have many many bats at Cabaña de Luz de Luna. But not eat the mosquito.'

'I expect they taste awful or give off a smell that bats don't like?' I said. 'Or the way they move? Or send out signals, maybe?'

Natalia smiled a 'who knows, who cares?' sort of smile and she responded in another way that was far more divine than the grasping *manos* hereabouts – or most-other-abouts for that matter. 'It is said among our people, that they are *'Hipnotizarlos…* it make the bats see ghosts.'

'They mesmerise the bats? How delightful a thought that is.' I gazed into those beautiful brown eyes, and she seemed not to be too much put off by my swollen face and blotchy body. Not for the whole morning, as we made the most of the gorgeously soft bed together. All beautiful morning.

She was so much more than a mine of information… a positive quarry of love and desire for the whole passionate time.

I only manage two holidays each year. A fortnight abroad, and the same in England. Always spoiling myself. So much pressure and hassle at work, I need to de-stress. What I really do not need is a trillion mosquitoes feasting on me and sticking me up with some awful poison. This fortnight in Costa Rica was supposed to be a nature awareness sort of spa break, up in the mountains, at a moderately civilised and comfortable lodge.

'It suits me perfectly,' I said, relaxing, stretched out on the patio lounger for the late afternoon. 'This summer warmth in the evenings, and this so-exotic, so-local fragrance, and you.' Natalia and I had bought the body cream on the *mercado local de productos agrícolas* that was held three days a week in the square. Chanelle Numero Uno, it said on the hand-written label. 'Mmm, it smells quintessentially local and interesting. Just matches my mood at the moment.' And promptly smeared ourselves in it.

That might have been a mistake, 'I think it's reacting with the mosquito juice,' I said to Natalia. 'I feel really weird. Like dizzy without falling over. All swimmy.'

'It strong stuff, Miss Madeleine. '

'I think you can call me Maddie, Natalia.'

'Yes, Miss Madeleine.'

I kept on feeling peculiar after Natalia had to go inside for an evening serving drinks behind the bar, but it was deliciously quiet out there in the suddenly-darkening gloom that brought a young man round lighting up the veranda lamps. He was nice, with a huge wide white smile and a little trolley of snacks and nibbles for retiring guests. But he wasn't for me. Ideally, I'd have a few tranquil hours sipping whatever local wine or liqueur was in the room's cocktail bar.

I thought the little expedition into the steamy forest yesterday evening was supposed to awaken the tourists' senses to the sights and sounds and smells of the jungly environment in the darkness? Didn't turn out so great for me, did it? Waylaid by marauding mozzies.

All that fake hush-hush stuff from the two guides, and warnings about spiders and snakes and things. So warm, humid; and faint moonlight under the canopy of black trees – I'm sure they fixed that. And there was me, batting away at insects the whole time. Dozens of great big whizzing ones; thousands of little zippy ones in the guide's flashlight, all around my head. And a veritable cloud swooping in and landing all over me. They just homed in on me like I was a long-awaited feast, stinging or biting or spraying or whatever they did to people's heads… and all the rest of them, too.

'I'm not going out with the group today,' I told the guide this morning. 'Not looking like this, all swollen up.' One of the others in our little group said she couldn't honestly see much difference, so I crossed her off my Christmas card list, and stayed in with Natalia. A much-improved day.

The two ladies from the room next to mine decided I needed company and a communal supper. They made it compulsory to try the black-bean soup and casado supper. 'It's reputed to have coca leaves soaked in it,' they giggled. 'You know,' so secretive, 'it's where cocaine comes from. They tell us it can be very strong.'

'Mind your bend... Or was it bend your mind, Lucy, dear?'

'Yes,' her companion agreed.

'Great, just what I need on top of a gallon of mosquito juice, a tub of Chanelle Numero Uno Cream – a litre of coke.' But it was tasty enough and I must have been quite peckish, because I slurped two dishes-full back and half a *pan dulce* loaf. Extra crusty. Washed down with three tazas gigantes of coca tea.

'Now that's funny,' I said, 'I can hear the bats; they're squeaking.' I watched them flittering around, catching flying insects, swooping close sometimes. 'It's quite a distinctive bleeping or chittering, as if they're in my head. It's a trifle irritating.' The bats came close, almost nipping and flicking at me. I hated things like that – they scare me. Might get in my hair or clothes, or scratch me, or poop on me. It hardly seemed worthwhile to wave at them, but I did. So I drank something else from the ladies' bottle and concentrated on telling the bats to go away.

I wished them away. Rather vehemently. Imagined them being afraid of me. Perhaps the coke was having an effect on me.

'It's worked,' Lucy told me. 'Look, they're staying further away.'

'I think you're right,' her friend Mimsy said, 'They seem to be staying more over the other side of the clearing now.'

'Perhaps I've mesmerised'em,' I laughed. 'Like the mosquitoes do.' And checked to see if there was any more black bean and coke soup.

The following day brought a multitude of torments. 'It's not the bats now,' I complained at lunch. 'It's every other damn thing. I can hear everything squeaking and whistling now – all the wi-fi signals, scraps of inane talking on people's mobiles – or cell phones, as they all call them in the Americas. There's a hiss, like a background signal or a television that's not tuned in. It's getting worse, like somebody keeps changing programmes; it explodes in my head.'

So we went for a walk with the guides in the afternoon, looking for massive insects and spiders, butterflies and tiny frogs. It wasn't very peaceful at all. Their Walky Talkies were driving me nutty. I was getting the whine of the signal as well as the jabbering of the two men – they were only discussing who they fancied in our group. It better not be me. Crude devils.

The evening television was a nightmare, 'I'm picking up fragments of other channels,' I complained to the others in our group. 'It's total confusion.' But they just looked and ignored me. Mad Maddie, as I heard someone mutter, before I fled to my room and concentrated on silence, quietening the buzzes and clicks and incessant chatter of idiot voices and banal television programmes. 'I need to get away from the receivers, or transmitters, whichever it is. God, I need them to be quiet.'

Wood and bamboo walls don't do much to soften incoming sounds; nor do the stone fireplaces, but gradually, between the repeat of the cocaine soup and the wine, the sounds seemed to deaden off, and I managed to sleep.

At breakfast in the morning, I ignored the chatter and consternation about signals being lost, mobile phones not working, the television wouldn't turn on, the guides' two-way radios didn't work. It would cause a lot of difficulties, they were moaning. 'Not for me,' I sniffed and went for a walk on my own, to a butterfly sanctuary about a mile along the main roadway. I listened out for noises in my head, tried to suppress them when they arose, and thought I was learning to control the constant background mishmash of the ether.

By evening, I was sufficiently recovered from the whole blood-polluting, head-filling nightmare to join another night-time walk. They sort of insisted – my ladies-next-door. The tiger insects hovered around. They focused on me again. 'I'm ready for you this time,' I warned them, 'You're not getting me again. I'm having *you*.'

Now that was totally out of this world – it was a lovely few minutes, sensing the panic among the swarm as it whirled and buzzed all round me. And broke up, dissipating into the night. I was really satisfied about that, and brushed my hands together, really theatrically. 'That works,' I said. 'I feel so much better.'

The local doctor came to check me over, at the insistence of my holiday company insurance. It was agreed that there was no long-term harm caused by the tiger insects' attention, subject to 'a few blood tests and a couple of days taking it easy.'

So no more rain forest walks for me. Had to suffer an unending supply of cocaine soup, cocktails, nibbles and Natalia in and around my room with the tub of All-over Body Cream. Over the course of the following days, I noticed the televisions were quieter, less confusing. 'It's like I can tune my head into one channel and ignore all the rest,' I told Natalia.

'I think it what *you* do,' Natalia stroked delicately. 'You are Mujer Tigre, Mother of the Tiger. You are Moyotzahuitl, wife of Tezcatlipoca, God of Smoking Mirrors. I hear many people in Lodge very cross because no can change televisions or make call on phone. Is you?'

What an interesting thought that is. Could it be? I could certainly try to make things quieter. So I experimented in my efforts, focusing on subduing some particularly noisy channels, as well as everybody's mobile phones. They're on holiday, for Samsung's sake.

I thought I was succeeding in controlling it. 'I'm just quietening it down,' I convinced myself, 'except for that godawful shrieking manic channel in Spanish that simply doesn't deserve to be on the air.' And it wasn't; the reception in the hotel faded.

'Not detect signal,' the engineers told the staff. 'Is still on air. It fade to nothing. *Nada.*'

The second part of the holiday, at a lodge on the coast, with a lovely beach, would be a welcome change of scene. I absolutely knew I'd miss Natalia, but it was quiet on the long coach trip down there – The coach radio wasn't working, nor anyone's mobiles. The beach lodge would be so peaceful for the scheduled five days. Solitude. Bliss. Away from the noise and clatter of incessant wi-fi. The staff were all mystified about the loss of radio and television signals. No wi-fi. The private helicopter bringing in a very posh-looking couple had landed very heavily with disruption to its communications and control systems. 'Oh dear. Was that me? It was very noisy in its electronics, as well as that awful engine.'

'Is it me? Making the signals quieter? Like suppressing them a bit? Really? Can I? On, or off? I think it must be me doing it... I mustn't think about this... or that... *or the other*.' I had to laugh.

It was very peaceful resting there at the Casitas Manuel: no television, no-one screeching endlessly into mobile phones. Sure, the actual people made as much noise as ever, but there wasn't all the wi-fi buzzing and shrilling all round me. The beach only had the sound of little waves and kids, and sellers of coconuts and T-shirts. Evenings were so peaceful, with the non-sound of televisions, CDs, radios and iTunes players. The gardens were alive with the sound of insects – but they seemed to keep well away from me. And the bats had all left the roof spaces, it seemed. Bliss.

I would so dearly have loved to stay on a few more days. I wasn't feeling confident enough to go into the Big Wide World, with all its screaming saturation of etheric noise. If it truly was something of my doing, I didn't think I was up to being overwhelmed. Kept sensing hints that there was more to this, like some lurking power, or curse, inside me. Perhaps something I'd barely tweaked yet. 'Maybe it will fade away if I stay longer,' I told the gecko that resided silently in my room. 'I can't control it, can't stop it. Something's going wrong every day – the meals are cold because the micro-waves don't work. The blinds wouldn't close… then won't open. The revolving doors are stuck. I really need to stop doing this, or learn to control it. If it truly is me doing it?

'Can I stay longer?' I asked. 'I'll pay, of course.'

But I couldn't remain there, the rep told me. 'The company can't alter flight bookings without a strong medical reason that the insurance would cover. We need you to be out the country before the insurance expires, Miz Tyler. No, you can't pay privately – the rooms are fully booked. And local accommodation really isn't safe, especially for a young woman alone. So I'm afraid it's the next shuttle bus to the airport.' Greaseball. All smarms one minute, till he found I lean the other way, and I gave his lady colleague the eye. So much more attractive than he was.

A mere three-hour drive along the coast road without fatalities. True, the radio with its blaring native rock music went strangely silent, but that was all. I resisted the urge to shut the driver up, with his constant yappering on his mobile. Until he swerved violently on a corner because he was swapping hands on his phone. Then I had to dampen it down, close it. Blessed electronic silence. Half the bus-full was complaining about the sudden lack of reception, checking their batteries, complete lack of any signal. So soothing on the nerves.

The airport was a nightmare of cacophonous sounds and tingles – such powerful signals penetrating me. *Lordy-Dee, it's so tempting to quieten them. No, I mustn't… Well, just him, maybe, still wittering on to his wife on his mobile, all lovey-dovey. Lying hypocritic. I'll take sleeping pills now. And some more before the flight. It wouldn't do to get excessively irritated in mid-air. I'll have a couple more during the flight – knock myself out…*

'England will be bliss, it's so quiet in Little Ploddingham. If this keeps up, I'll be able to quieten incoming wi-fi signals, including that new chappie who's moved in next door, always on his mobile at the top of his voice, and got Netflix on at a million decibels half the night. Maybe I can drive the bats out of my roof space – nasty acid-crapping loft-destroyers protected by more sodding laws than kids are. No, no. Mustn't get annoyed, I'd probably switch the radar off or air traffic control or something. Calm yourself, Madeleine Tyler. Relax.'

It was a terribly long wait at the airport, but it gave me time to get my thoughts together. 'I could perhaps find out where Sky and all that lot broadcast from. Pay their studios a visit. London would probably come to a disastrous halt if the studios are there. Wouldn't be any harm done, though, if London was to close down for a day or two. *It would only be like a snowfall shutting it all down.*

'Or perhaps I might learn to direct this. Increase the distance? If I could close down all the French channels, and the Dutch ones – they're *such* irritating creatures.'

The screens came up with our flight back to Heathrow: another hour before boarding. 'Certainly, all the wi-fi noise isn't as overpowering and frightening as it was at first. Still not entirely predictable, though. I need to be so careful on the plane. It's going to be a ten-hour flight. I'll take an extra dose of the sleeping pills. Warn them I'm a heavy sleeper so they won't try to wake me up.'

It took ages to get through security – those irritating X-ray machines packed up and the staff eventually had to search about twenty passengers' cabin baggage by hand. And frisk all the people, too.

But the plane was comfortable, and I had a window seat, by myself. The unoccupied seat next to me was a welcome surprise. 'So no-one will be disturbing me with pathetic attempts at conversation.'

Overhead locker closed up; settled on my own. Two more pills; blanket around me and pillow against the window… Dreamy days… Perfect flight.

Lord, my dream was so intense. I was warm and wriggling all over… Positively writhing… So intense…

So much. Not had a lover like this… squirming. Feel myself moaning. Lord, that was something else! Wowsy! This was a lover like nobody since Ivana.

43

Lordy! She'd been something else. My, we'd loved so much, so hard, so intense. Lke this…

But. It was dawning on me… *This isn't a dream!* Realisation. The noise. 'I'm on a plane. Ivana and I split months ago. *What's happening?'* I forced my eyes open, the dream still uppermost. Looking around. Not understanding. A man!!!! So close, cuddling next to me. His hand was moving inside my clothes. *God!!! Down there!!!! Nooooo!!!* He was whispering to me, murmuring. His fingers still massaged and probed.

'Gerroff me!!!' I panicked. Screamed. Shrieked. Lashed out. 'Get away!!! Who are you? Get off.' I pushed and hit and shouted, 'You filthy mauling creature—'

People turned. Some stood, stared. 'He's attacking me!!! Mauling me!!! I don't know him. Get him away from me!!! Get him off me!!!'

No-one moved. I was half asleep still. Freaking out. Announcements coming over from the cabin staff, 'All remain seated… Coming in to land. Final approach. Passengers must remain seated.' They wouldn't come to me… Ignoring me.

This bastard was smirking again, saying, 'What's your problem, eh, girl?' His hand groped back onto my leg…

I shrieked more and louder and battered at him. Scratched and tore at his face. The plane lurched on one side. *Everybody* screamed then: *You're not going to ignore me just like that.*

He half-fell out his seat – *my* spare seat. I could feel the throwing about-ness of the plane. We dropped and rolled and toppled over. Big lurch and a swing. And like a great drop. There was this stink of puke everywhere. The vile man went flying up. And down. He kept hitting the ceiling… and went flying down towards the front and battered himself around. All arms and legs and screaming everywhere. I hated hated hated him. Disgusting beast. He came tumbling back and was all covered in blood all the way down to the rear. And he was on the ceiling again. He made all bloody smears on it, and his face was all terror and horror and he smashed into the back of the plane again and rolled over and over…

I think I read somewhere that 747s can do a barrel roll when they're being tested. This one apparently did two, one each way. Plus a vertical stall whilst attempting to perform a loop. We went falling backwards and doing something called a screwroll; apparently.

On the news, they mentioned a negative gravity roll as being something *extremely* unusual for a large passenger aircraft. I think that was like a loop on the outside. That was when *everybody* was sick. And other things, too.

We sort-of-landed in a great cloud of sparks and smoke and lots of foam.

What heroes pilots are.

Eventually, someone came to me to ask about the screaming immediately before the flight crew lost all control. I told them, 'It wasn't just the pilots who lost all control. Most other passengers lost control of their bowels, bladders and stomachs. It was all the fault of that revolting man came and sat next to me… groping me. Horrible creature.'

'He was very badly injured.'

'Good. If he's still alive, he's not injured enough. He's the one who caused it all.'

The aircraft will reportedly need at least a week to clean it, if they bother. It's being assessed as a write-off, because of the damage sustained during the belly-flop landing at around three hundred miles per hour. The fire service had *so* much more excitement than ever before. The pilots are in need of counselling. People's phone videos from inside the plane and from the ground have reached a hundred million hits on YouTube already. Boeing are baffled, and all 747s have been grounded for an estimated six weeks. 'Huh. Again?' I said. 'Silly things, planes. Nasty people on them.'

Mr Creepy Handy will not face any charges for his vile sexual assault on me. 'He has suffered life-changing injuries,' they're telling me at the police headquarters. It's a man in a suit who's smarming at me. He thinks he's somebody important in the CPS; and a woman police officer in a uniform-type posh top and skirt.

'Life-changing injuries? So what? Is that supposed to make any difference to me? He probably had a really slimy-crawly life that needed to be changed. You're making me a tad peeved, the way you're acting, all full of sympathy for Creepy Handy. *I'm* the victim here, not that slimeball.'

'It would serve no purpose to charge him. It would not be in the public good.' The patronising man and the slithery lady are smiling. Unctuous creeps, 'But he can't

46

claim compensation because he should have had his seat belt fastened. He was not even in his own seat when the plane's troubles began.'

'That's what I'm telling you,' I'm shrieking at them. 'It definitely would be in the public interest: it would be in *my* public interest. *He attacked me!!! He was in the seat next to me with his hand in my knickers!*'

Perhaps I shouldn't call them CPS Suits… morons… misogynists… lesbian-haters… and everything else, but I'm cross with them. I'm *very* cross with them. I can only take so much.

Now the lights are flickering. And fading. And going right out. This interview room's dark now, and the microphones are dead. All the recording equipment is slowing down. And it's stopped. 'Ooo! That made me jump.' The computer next to me just went click. And it smells somewhat, er, *burny.*

Somebody's coming in. It's dark out there as well, and he's hardly even a silhouette. 'The phones aren't working; nor are the mobiles. We have to evacuate.'

So we started to work our way along the passage and down the stairs and I'm telling them, 'This makes no difference. You can't use this as an excuse. Creepy Hands must be charged.'

'Do give it a rest, luv,' one's answering me, so condescending. 'We have much more important things to bother about.'

Well! Calling *me*, "Luv".

'And what's more important than me?' I ask him, just as we arrive at the bottom of the stairs where there's some daylight. 'Me and Justice?'

'Do shut up, missus. You've had your answer. It's not in the public interest.'

47

Silly man, talking to an affronted member of the public in that disrespectful and dismissive manner. *Silly* man.

Now a policeman in uniform is coming over. 'The CCTV cameras have gone off.'

'So have the televisions and the monitors,' a baffled-looking skinny lad is saying. I stand there and listen while he's telling them, 'The internet went down. The heating's making funny clicking noises. And... well, just *everything's* stopped.' He looks baffled and they're all rather worried.

'Never mind all this,' I start to say, 'What about my horrid man and him being charged with—'

'Go away.'

'So that's your attitude at the CPS, is it?' I say. And I get ignored. So I go storming across the big foyer. 'I can only take so much of this. You definitely ought to charge him,' I'm shouting at everybody. 'You *really* should. I'm still *exceptionally* cross about it. It will be *so* much better for the public good when he is charged.' I stamped my foot very hard to let them know I was *really* cross.

The lights across the road are flickering, and going off, leaving the shops in murky darkness. The traffic lights aren't working. And some cars can't seem to get started going again.

I'm very cross, walking towards the tube station. 'It'll be *so* much better for the public good when you bring charges against him.

'I can feel this escalating no end. I can only take so much.'

I KEEP HAVING BLACKOU—

'I had another blackout yesterday, Mi Duck.'

Pekin-Cayuga – as I call her – sniffed, 'Shush, Emmerdale's just starting.'

'I keep having'em. Getting more frequent. Yesterday, I was watching some programme by that Attenborough feller, about wild cats, and I thought I must have dozed off. So I rewound it, and I'd completely missed about two minutes.'

She wasn't listening; she was off with the Dingles.

'Then it happened again today.' I don't give up easily, though Emmerdale or Coro always win in the end. 'I was in the garden,' I told her, 'and I suddenly had no recollection of pruning that ginkgo in the corner. But I'd trimmed back a dozen overlong shoots. They're underlong now.'

Tuesday morning, the same. I had another dead spell, standing at the bus stop. I missed the 7.50 and the 8.05. Made me twenty minutes late to work. 'You're going to have to watch out for this, Harold,' my boss warned me. 'Can't have this getting to be a habit.'

Course, the doc hadn't got an appointment for three days. 'Now, *that's* a touch worrying,' I told Jerimiah The Cat. 'I worry about the NHS sometimes.'

Then again – One minute I was chatting with Pete Next Door, and I shook my head and had no idea what he'd just been saying. Something boring. Probably about their yappy dog. Next minute, he's asking if I'm alright. 'You stood there motionless for a minute or more. Gone, you were. I kept waving a hand in front of you, and calling you. Then you came back… It was as if somebody pinched your mind for a minute,' he told me. 'Totally gone. You sure weren't here.'

So I rang 111 – the non-emergency-but-bloody-worrying number and they told me to ring 112. *They* practically laughed and said I was a time waster and should go to A&E if I was worried. I said, 'I daren't drive.'

And they said it didn't warrant an ambulance and I should go to my GP.

And I said, 'He doesn't have any appointments until Friday.'

So on Friday, I was sitting in the waiting room – half an hour behind on appointments as usual, and the next thing I knew some woman was tapping me and saying 'Is that you? Your name on the screen? That's twice they've called you.'

'There's nothing wrong with you.' The doc smugly informed me before he even started on the blood pressure, pulse rate, height and weight, lung capacity, then got on to abdominal tightening, on the spot exercises, and some quick mental questions, before repeating, 'There's nothing wrong with you, but if you're still worried, I'll take some blood for testing. You can go for an EEG scan this afternoon at the Walker Street Clinic. It'll take ten days to get the results back, so make an app…'

That was the last thing I heard. That surprised him, except he thought I was acting the fool, and was pretty irritated with me by the time I came round. 'I might have epilepsy or psychogenic somethings, Doctor. I'm clearly not drunk, and my blood looks well oxygenated, and you just told me I'm not on any contra-medications.'

So I was at Walker Crescent at 3.00 p.m. and they rigged me up with wires and sticky bits everywhere. Half an hour later, they checked the readings. There was a dead four-minute patch in the middle. 'This is the reading we'd get off a corpse,' the technician told me, really supportively.

So, with nothing better to do, and dying to play with their new £8,000 toy plus extra software they decided to experiment with possible causes – bright lights, flickering lights, high-pitched squeaks, squawks, low drones, needle pricks, electric contacts... *Nothing.* I told'em, 'You should try me on blue cheese, chocolate and alcohol. They might be the trigger.'

'Interesting,' they said, and kept me on the bed for another hour, and a nurse sat and watched me while I'm wired up to another dozen monitors – pulse, BP, ECG... But the nurse fell asleep and didn't see what I was doing when my cut-off happened again. Six minutes dead.

They got me back into the monitoring suite next day. I was half an hour late – doesn't time fly sometimes? And they had me on some kind of MRI scanner. 'Functional magnetic resonance,' White-Coat One said, very sagely. 'Plus a pair of cameras. We don't want people dying in here and coming back to life. Not without us understanding it, anyway. Do you mind if we get a group of students in? You'll be a good little study for them.'

Five minutes later there were thirteen of us in there. With me answering a few dim-student questions whilst they checked me over and fitted me up. And, 'Yes, I think I had a couple more episodes during the night at home – once eating my supper. It was gone without me noticing anything. I thought my wife took it away, but I didn't know if I ate any of it.' They all looked at me like I was Hair-brain Harold. 'And the other one, judging from the cat's wide-eyed and ears-back yowling, had been when we'd gone to bed. Sometime in the night, I woke on top of the covers. Stark naked, so I must have walked round in my sleep.'

After an enthusiastic initial interest, the students went off the boil and half of them were texting or surfing. Until one of the technicians manning the apparatus, started tapping the equipment and adjusting the wiring, and his colleague was poking at me, as if making sure I was still there. Muttering and puzzling in jargon about I had an adiabatic fast passage and resonance inversion combined with zero-filling interpolations. Something like that.

'The contrast dropped around four percent, on the cameras.' White-coat One explained.

'But we don't believe there's anything wrong with the gear, or the readings.' WC2 was still poking at the dials. 'We're re-checking all the calibrations.'

'We thought it was *you* who faded,' one of the spotty students piped up, and was promptly hushed.

'We pretended that was why we were poking at you.' The cheeky-faced little blonde one sniggered.

'The EEG showed all your brain activity suddenly stopped,' White-coat Two re-joined the discussion, 'for forty-eight seconds, exactly when you seemed to have partially faded away. 'Readings show your blood pressure had frozen still, heart stopped, no breathing.'

'You were dead. Forty-eight seconds. It's as though your mind had gone – total absence of activity.'

'Not much change there, according to my missus – and it's *her* who watched Emmerdale.'

'And some of your body had gone with it.'

'Precisely 4.1016 percent.' WC2 rechecked his figures.

'It was as if you'd gone a bit see-through,' a quite-dishy studenty lass said.

'All my mind, and part of my body? It's a *proper* mystery, isn't it?' I sort of goaded them for self-entertainment.

'Not a *part* of you... more accurately, a *percentage* of you.'

'You had sort of... er, thinned out.'

'Become less substantial.'

'Are you an alien?'

'Aren't students wonderful?' I said to White-coats One and Two.

The registrar led them in a discussion of what they would need to know and observe to determine whether or not I was an alien... or if a proportion of me really had miraculously vanished for a moment. *She can't be taking the idea seriously!*

The main thing she needed, it was astutely decided, would be more tests. And my complete medical history, 'If you have one?'

'Course I have.' I was affronted at that. 'Cheeky moo. I was born a mile away, been registered at the Church Avenue Medical Centre ever since. They'll have all my records – plus my mum's and dad's. I'm as normal as you lot.' I looked round the students. 'More than most of you.'

Then they sent for *The Consultant*. 'He's exceptionally erudite,' they said. But he had no more idea than anybody else, although he asked the students and his registrar all sorts of questions to guide their wonderings. I'm lying on the bed in a theatre gown and—

—and they're all agog and gabbling away and got their phones out taking pics of me – lying there naked. 'Ay-up,' I said, 'Put'em away. I'm starkers.'

My gown had gone. It was underneath me. The wires and pads were off, too. I was lying on them. 'What happened? Did all of me vanish for a second?' I'm trying not to be too obvious about covering myself up, but it's not easy when you are actually stark bollock and they're all snappy-happy.

'No, not *one* second,' they delightedly informed me. 'Four minutes.'

'And you were *gone*, body and mind. Total.'

'You disappeared, and your gown just flopped down, like it was deflated.' Blondie demonstrated with puffy cheeks and falling hands.

'I don't know where you've been, but you weren't here…' The consultant informed me; rather haughtily, I thought.

'Doctor Kota was feeling all over the bed; she didn't believe it. Just as well she'd taken her hands away when you popped back…'

'I was holding my breath… almost counting, expecting you back any second.'

'You sure you're not an alien trying to *Go Home?*'

'Y' pack of silly sods.' I told'em. 'Bloody students.'

They were all laughing, sort of nervously, and keeping a bit further back. So I pulled the gown out from under me and dragged it back on while the students debated and disbelieved and reviewed the evidence on their mobiles; and the consultant and registrar mumbled about late for lunch; and White-coats One and Two poked and re-calibrated and mentioned phase encoding gradients while they replayed their squiggles.

I mean, I felt fine, except it was a bit worrying. 'Do you really suppose I could be an ET type – bright green, with great big eyes, long neck and no dick?' I asked the consultant, and peeked inside the gown to re-check.

They managed to rewind the room-cam, and – 'Yep, see. The cameras don't lie.' They replayed the whole thing. 'See? You weren't there. The whole of that time.' It was a bit scary, actually. I really had just vanished off the padding, with my gown and wires flopping flat.

'We need to get the weight monitors under you. The sort we use to keep a check on long-term bed-bound cases.'

They were easing even further away from me, as if they'd catch something. 'We need to analyse all the data we've gathered... consult together.'

'In private.'

That was obviously so they could admit they were baffled and not show themselves up in front of me, the nurses and the two radiologist-technician-white-coat bods.

They trooped out and left the nurses to find a patient-in-bed weigher. Back in two minutes flat, the nurses were cackling, 'We nicked the Detecto from GW stores,' they said, and rolled me on one side, laid a mat under me, and rolled me back the other way to get it straight. Checking the calibration to zero, they eventually left it to the technicians, who happily busied themselves refitting my wires and sticky pads.

Right, I'm thinking: *First, this is getting more frequent; second, they haven't got a clue; third, they're imagining I'm playing tricks on them – their own mass hysteria or something; and fourthly: that last time, I had a vague impression of something occurring during those four minutes.*

'I think I saw face-like things,' I told the nurses. 'They might have been big-eyed, or perhaps got goggles on. Wiggly mouths.'

'You've been listening to too many alien-minded students,' the nurses dismissed me. They clearly weren't going to pay attention to such newly-invented drivel from me, so I addressed the two technicians, 'What is this? Have you transferred me to some experimental lab in Area 51 while I was away with the… fairies? I was seeing something bright, all shifting, as though I was seeing it through swirling water. And there were some sounds, Japanese –type music, all weird and ghastly… or ghostly, similar to some Gagaku stuff in a NipponHK travel doc I was watching the other week.'

They looked at each other and stepped a little further away, 'The cameras are still on,' they warned me. 'Mind what you say, or they'll have you in the looney bin.'

Buggerit, I was in deep do-dos here. The more I strained to recall anything, the more I was getting an impression of… *someone.* Something had been looming over me. Weird Close Encounters-type faces. Perhaps trying to touch me, feel at me. The weirdo Jap sounds might have been made by them, not just floating in the air. Fruckerty-foo – if you had a voice that sounded like drifting flutes and a banjo being plucked at a tenth the usual rate. *Soddit, this's getting creepy. I'm definitely not dreaming.* I resisted the urge to pinch myself – I never could imagine what good that would do.

The nurses and apparatus duo kept popping back and assuring me, while they wandered round with coffees and sheets, coils of wire and headsets. 'You're okay, you're definitely alive; all the readings are fine…'

'You're looking good; healthy…'

White-coat One peered up from his readings. 'Apart from keeping vanishing, of course.'

'What do you mean,' I sat up. '"*keeping* vanishing"? It's only happened the once.'

'Er, no. Twice more in the past half-hour. We've messaged Mr Clitheroe, but he and his firm are holding one their review-lunches. They can take some time. We just laid the covers over you, and slotted the main headset on. We thought, if you're going to keep doing it, we'd better keep a spare sheet handy...'

'*I* don't keep doing it – *it* keeps doing it to me. I'm not long for this world, then?'

They looked shocked that I would say such a thing, but then realised I meant it literally… and sort of laughed. Glanced at each other. Seemed a tad nervous.

'And the Detecto shows twelve-stone-six lighter for each period. That's the whole of you.'

'All the readings all zeroed out, too.'

'Away with the fairies again, was I?'

It's happened another time now, and I was ready for it, almost. Mostly surprised that it had come just about when I was expecting it – a dream waiting for me. I just knew I'd be in that dream place again. And the little buggers in the dream seemed very real. They were ready for me, too, trying to speak directly to me in that fluty-banjo noise. I got the impression they were desperate to get something over to me. *Mentally pressuring me.* I thought, and poking fingery things into me, the same as the students had been doing. *They're after something... wanting something from me... seemed very eager...*

I could see the readout on the Detecto weighing screen – little green digits – "12st: 2lb." *Eh? That means I've lost five pounds in the past half-hour. Maybe I didn't all come back? I'm thinning out.* White-coats were puzzling over the accuracy of the readouts, not what they meant, and only grunted without hearing when I asked about it.

'Something in their weird sounds seemed familiar,' I was telling the nurses. 'Almost conveyed some meaning to me. I think I must be getting used to it.' But I don't think these two nurses care all that much. They never looked up from their texting, anyway. Perhaps they'd understand if I talked in Japanese Gagaku tones? Or adopt a silly high-pitched voice and sing the "Ying Tong" song?

Well, I'm lying here with these four, plus the cameras, 'Not going to offer me anything to eat or drink?' I asked, ages ago. I'm sure they don't understand English... *Unless it's me who's not speaking English any longer?*

'Hey, that's a worrying thought...' But I checked – I said a silly tongue-twister about Mrs Hunt – it could never be translated into Weirdo Nipponese, so I must still be speaking English.

Anyway, I reckon I've had two more in the last ten minutes. It's not as though the machine beeps or anything, and the two techies have gone off for a break… the nurses are nattering and texting… and I saw the weight readout – 11st: 1lb. 'That's more than another stone! They're getting better at keeping bits of me.' But they weren't going to look up from their phones.

The way things have been going, a couple more decent blackouts should do it. So the docs and students won't have anybody to gawp at when they get back from lunch.

That'll really give'em something to think abou—

INTO THE ARENA

Frugging waste of time, this is. I should be fighting, learning, strengthening. *Must* be better, faster. Weapons hall is boring with no-one to fight. I useless without sword or axe, and an enemy to slash and crush. This is first time in the daylight I've been left to myself.

'Today you rest,' Captain Godrun tell me. 'Tomorrow – arena.'

My wounds mend fast; learn their speech; practise to fight every day since they drag me from swamp and brought me to Great House.

'Ritual combat,' they say. 'On the morrow. Staged battle. Symbolic.'

'Symbolic death?' I said.

'No. The death is real. You are the Backman to Lord Rogor. You *must* fight.'

Yesterday, Godrun was desperate to make me fight, train me. He vicious. Hate me, want me dead more than he want me fit to fight in arena.

Outside, in courtyard, we fight every day. Throw ourselves at each other. Do best to hurt. Not cripple or kill. 'We need you for the arena, Kyre. If you're still alive after that, I *will* kill you.'

'Join queue,' I tell him.

But today, this morning. 'No more,' he said. 'You rest on your last day.'

'Because tomorrow I die?' It was stupid to bother saying it. We know I be dead in the arena with Lord Rogor. Captain Godrun and family will all be at the mercy of Sandor's army. I not like Godrun, or Wifey very much. But sorry about daughter Wisty. She is koh. I never touch her, but make him mad to think I did. More mad he is, more it make him train me harder. Need to be as good as I can be.

So this day I must spar with myself. I rant, build up my fury to bring on my star-sent speed to turn the direction of the fight. But it never come again – not when I want. I *must* find the trigger to make it come in the arena. But we have not found what sparks me into a whirling blade in past ten days. So now I stab and slash at uniforms and armoured racks in vain. I will die without my speed. Tomorrow. Noon.

My arms are strong; move well. The sharpest pains have faded, the cuts and bruises, the crushed fingers and cracked ribs. Not last much longer. I go back whence I came. No loss.

My body frugg-all use: need more skill, and more *faster*. No use if slow like other men. Maybe dying not too bad – army camp troopers manage it koh. I kill them quick. They not laugh at me now. Hope it like that for me. Die quick.

My life empty – half in hound cage coming from swamp to Great House. Then here – ten days with axes, lances, swords. This hall same as my sleeping room – no place to sleep and live. Like me – just a weapon. Everywhere – uniforms, leather and armour… Shields and banners; huge swords. Godrun's idea of life. Fighting here, and in army camps… or near-die in wagon with the hounds. Ha, maybe I not made to last. Find out on morrow.

The old woman who treated my wounds last time was at the door; she from the Rua Sisterhood. 'We'll share a few words, Kyre.'

She sat me down by the battered mogg-wood table, stood behind me, and held my head in her hands. As on other days, her fingers flexed on the split in my skull, murmuring under her breath. Some of the words I have heard so many times from the other sisters of the Rua. 'Unity… Safety. Have faith. Unity of the Realm.' And new ones now, 'You must search inside yourself. It will arise in you. Do what you feel.'

'I feel like running away,' I said. 'Want to be not-me. Safe then. You're Snota, they say?'

'I am Hutor Rua, Snota the Wise.'

'I get four names from you. But some tell me no name.'

'Perhaps I am four times more than they are.' Her hands stilled over the split in my head. 'Except Rua Li, whom you met. I am only twice what she is. Hutor is my title – Leader. Be strong for the Realm. Li was right about you.'

'Right what?' I tried to turn to look at her but her hands clutched tightly into my head.

'You are very different, Kyre. You have power within like I have never felt before. Rua Li must be especially sensitive to have sensed your specialness from so far away. And such extreme dedication and determination to immediately mend the worst of your wounds... to orient your mind... to entwine with you, for your seed.'

They use so many words I not understand. Not sure what she meant: we had entwined, yes, in the furs, in the compound where we killed the hill bandits. But *my seed?* What is that?

'Suddenly, Kyre-*bruyot,* we dare to hope. If you survive the contest against Sandor's troop, we may start to believe our prayers have been heard. You may be a step along The Pathway to the future of the realm, though the great power inside you is buried... hidden and damaged by this terrible injury to your head... and the infections from all the deep wounds.

Her fingers massaged into the deep gashes in my head and my side. We very much prefer that you live through the morrow. The prospect of Lord Sandor's victory is not something to contemplate with joy. For him to become Lord of the Rangelands would be a terrible blow to our dreams for the realm.

How strange are her words. What does prospect mean? Contemplate? Dedication? 'Rua Li said you were *secret* group? But I have seen four of you?'

'We are secret, but as you will be dead tomorrow, I can tell you. *No, don't go!* I jest. You know I am senior Rua – *The Hutor.* We are five here in Lordstown. You have the marks on your wrist, given by Sisters Li and Ravena; they warrant that you are worthy of our attention. This third one *here* is mine.'

I stared at the small tattoos that have appeared on my wrist during the past days. 'A flapping bollock?'

I had to smile at the sudden stilling of her fingers on my shoulders. 'The winged eye that sees all.' She said it so coldly. 'Be still, some of these gashes are deep, infected. You should not train and fight so hard.'

'I must. And must fight more hard on morrow. Yes?'

'Yes. For the realm.'

Whether caused by her bony-fingered massaging into my back and head, her ceaseless incantation, or her urgings to swallow the foul drink, I felt new strength flood through me and I calm. Her hands ceased their pressing and probing, and left me. I waited, but she said no more.

Perhaps I slept for a time.

I turned. She was gone. At the end of the hall, Godrun, Wifey and Wisty were at their noon-day meal. They looked up as I stood, and stared at me as though I had returned from the grave. I hesitated, hoping Wisty would invite me to join them awhile, as on other days. But Godrun turned to them, muttering.

'I'll go,' I said, attempting a superior shrug, and tried to swagger to my own room. *Only one more evening I live. When I return to my non-time, my time unknown, before the swamp, I not miss them.* I crashed the door closed, in temper, and turned to my empty room.

Not the bare void I expect.

The wondrous Rua girl stood there. She with the beauteous naplewood hair. The silverline scar on her cheek. I stared. And trembled. *Why has she come?* 'Hi,' I said. 'You not tell me your name before.'

'I waited for you.' She was approaching, perhaps as nervous as I. A smile on delicate features. So close, her slender fingers took hold of her flower-embroidered jackette and lifted a little. I trembled as she lifted her top, exposing the twin goddesses of her breasts. A swift, slinking movement, and the covering was gone. 'I like the way you look at me, Kyre. You make me feel... *powerful*. How I've not felt for many a season. No need for names.'

Standing, helpless, I shivered as slender fingers slipped inside my shirt. 'Ufff,' I sucked in, eyes closing unbidden. I writhed – those fingers stroking me! Toying at my nipples. Nails raking me in divine gentleness. 'Jeemus, Lady...'

I must reach back, to explore. She tensed and quivered under my touch. *I must be doing the same to her.* Meeting her eyes, pressing close to me, her lips parting, meeting mine, and pressing, squirming against me. *Liot and Dirith!* Her tongue entering my mouth. I was responding, everywhere.

After long joyful moments, she teased away, a playful smile, breathing deeply as we each slipped off

68

our remaining clothes, and recommenced our stroking and delving. As if by mutual magic, tormenting, so tantalizing. The lightest of touches, of massages, as if knowing exactly. The head-filling scent of hedgerow blossoms in her hair…

She shuddered. Nervous as I. There was an urgency as I touched her, so softly tender, fluttering and gasping. *'Dirith*, Lady, you are the stars. So much I need you.'

She took the lead, and held my hand to the bed. *She knows what I must do. Will guide me. But! – Godrun and family must know of this. Will be imagining… Ahh, let them; Kyre hte cufk.*

My ecstasy knew no bounds; as though transported among the clouds in warmth and feelings I never knew existed. On this day of pending terror, could I have dreamed of such?

The entwinement! The Glory of her body… her movements. This, I would remember forever… Until the noonday sun tomorrow.

'You haven't eaten today. Come; we'll find something.' She led me along a corridor and down a flight of unlit stone stairs. 'This is the lower servants' area.'

Laughter, chatter and clattering built up as we made our way down a long passageway, with dull-flickering side flames. Heading towards a brighter glow. New warmth and anticipation rose in me as we approached a bright and noisy hall. The same size as Godrun's training room, but this ceiling was lower, a wide kitchen, with a scullery and food preparation area, and a series of separate rooms and alcoves around the

69

white-stone walls. Such warmness... the aromas! An all-enveloping smell of hot bread filled me. My hunger suddenly roused. The sight of such undreamed foods scattered across the table-tops.

A dozen or more people sat or stood; relaxed, eating, talking. As many again were collecting food and drink to load onto a table that lifted through a chimney. Two motioned us aside so they could push their laden trolley past us. A brief smile. A couple of heads turned to see who had come in, but I saw no interest in them.

'Come see what there is,' my companion was at home here. 'We do the food for the high people in this kitchen; and our own house-staff food, too. I work here between other tasks I have. The soldiery have their own hall and canteen at the north end of the house – we don't mix much with the troopers. We can eat in here or take it back to your quarters. As you wish.'

I gazed at her, so slender and smooth in her movement as she talked me through the dishes on the long trestle table, some of them left-overs from the family tables. Laughing with a pock-faced girl, she helped herself to a small slice of meaty pie and offered me a large portion. 'We eat well, if strangely-mixed sometimes. Our own foods are put out here, too, with what is sent back from the tables of the Lord's rooms. See what you like the look of. Shall we sit?' I followed her to a bench seat by the scullery entrance, where the rich smell of a wood fire originated.

A few others noticed us... *me*... taller than all, the mess of scrapes and scars across my head. Picking unknowing at the food dishes, clad in leather training garb, so different to their dress. Two room staff were filling a tray to take upstairs for a guest. One called a jovial hello, 'Who's your new friend? Don't he know scirry from potted hound?' I attempted to curl small behind her, and tasted a mix of foods, but was soon ignored, comfortable with my companion. She explained, suggested, went back for different ones, and we joked about the taste and the weird mix they made; and a pretty girl coming past said we made a weird mix, too.

My nameless companion fended off a friend's prying about what she was up to these days, 'Going away again, eh? Who's this?'

'He's the big'un they had stripped off stark bollock a dodec back,' a man's voice was loud enough to be heard by all.

A woman jested back, 'Yes, and, as I remember, he's got a lot more than you have, Elmar, down there. So you needn't go on about it.'

'Even with half of it leaked out, he's also got more in his head than you have, Elmar.'

Elmar quietened, but came over moments later, apologising. 'It's been a busy day, getting ready for the tourney tomorrow, all the tables and food and visitors. Everything needed cleaning and all these out-land foods for the newcomers and visitors. We're sending supplies over for the additional troops they've drafted in to keep order. They'll make sure the change of lord goes smooth.'

'And suppose we win?' My naple-haired bedfriend laughed.

'What? With Lord Rogor the Volko barely off his sick bed? Three or four bloated bastiainen from the defence brigade to hide behind? And some other cunny they got locked away, doing nothing but snivel? Sure;

we'll stomp all over'em. Word is, Sandor's lot will have the marauder brigade in the arena. Fast attacking force. They're the ones who go in and slaughter a whole village in a dozen minins if somebody's been disrespectful to Sandor. They've been out practising on the fields the other side of the marsh most days. They can dress in light armour and run two hundred paces carrying any two weapons – in one groze beats! Our chubby scruggers'll still be strapping their dick-covers on.'

'Or wobbling up the hill.' Someone else laughed.

'We're all looking forward to the market and festival afterwards,' One of the servers joined in, 'and hope we'll still have jobs the day after. 'Some of us aren't thinking of being here tomorrow if Sandor's army's coming round. Big force, he's got. They'll be spoiling for it here – Lord's got treasures aplenty, and his kids'll have to go. The men'll be for the stake. And Susi and the little thing with the stupid name – they'll be frugged silly and chucked over the wall.'

A kitchen girl's smack across Elmar's face shut him up. 'Everyone's thinking the same, Elmar, but it don't need shouting about.'

'It's you, in't it? *You're* the Backman! Jeemo scrugging…'

Another man was coming towards us. 'Yes, it *is* you. I saw you in the courtyard, few days ago.' He turned to the others, 'He was shike.'

'I worse now.' I tried to laugh it off. 'Morrow, you drag selves out tavern, can watch me burn at the stake, koh? That be nice picnic for you, won't it? You can have smores.'

At least, that was what I thought I said, but the cackling made me wonder if I hadn't got some of the words quite right. 'I'll tell you later,' my friend-girl whispered. 'They just think you're badly injured in your head and are being sacrificed.'

'That right. Is that beer he got? I like beer.'

A moment later – a miracle from the stars – a beer jug appeared beside me. 'Anybody with a purple prick that size and a cunny bigger than my Adri's – on the side of his head! They get a drink from me any day!' He was one of the older servants, in uniform. Laughing, 'My gift, and good luck to ya, lad. You'll need it.' I think that was what he said.

He raised his glass; the others did the same, and my friend companion nudged me, 'Do the same.'

They all drank a sip, 'Good luck,' they all said, looking at me.

Inside, I felt emotion. Like not before. 'They really wish me well?'

My friend-girl with the silverline scar creased in half with laughter. 'They don't "have an inclination for your deep wet hole". They hope you will win. Just keep it up, Backman Kyre. They hope you have good luck.'

There was something in the way she said it. I said, 'You think, "For a day".'

Her face became red. 'I did, I'm sorry. Have one more beer and we'll go. It's not good to have a lot of beer. No, it doesn't matter if you're dead tomorrow after noon. Too much of this would be bad for you in the morning.'

I shrug. *It not matter to me.*

Taking the long passageways back up to Godrun's quarters, she came into my room, and stopped by the foot of the bed. 'Tell me your name,' I said.

'No.'

'Koh, Scarface, I'll just have to…' She went stiff, took a step back. Upset. 'They call me Kyre, but it's not my name. It just means "question".

'Yes, Greatmother Snota told me you speak like the Doronian people in Broganta – they begin with a word to express their emotion or purpose – like jest, command or question, so there is no mistake. She also said that deep inside, you carry the name Th'*ron*? But here, you are *Kyre*.'

I not certain I understood all she said, but she had a lovely voice and her loose blouse quivered delightfully when she spoke so intensely. 'Koh. Tell me any name you like the sound of.'

'Graleen was my mother. Graleese and Karina are my daughters.' She lowered her head as if shy about it.

'Koh,' I decided. 'You're the mother now, so you are Graleen. Koh? Call me whatever you want. It only for a day.'

'No!! You must not speak thus!! We Rua have much hope for you. Let Captain Godrun despair. Not you. Not Rua.'

'Ha, you make me laugh; hope will not help us. Need fast speed. It not come.' I sat on the bed, and patted the pillow beside me, to invite her. She came and started to lift her top, but I stop her, 'We talk, eh? Your man?'

'Stirior died. After Karina, my daughter, was born. And I took this' she touched a finger down her scarline. 'He was a guardsman at the festival of Midsummer.

Rebel men came to kill the old lord. The attackers were all killed, then, or later. You've seen the bare patches in the arena centre? Around the posts where there's ash from other burnings? They always get burned there. The rebels screamed a lot, and I liked that.' She touched her cheek again, and was silent for an age. Until she said, 'After, I had no man. So I had to leave. We were very hungry, my two little girls. The Rua gave me chance of more life. Now, my children will have laughter in their eyes, not bleak starvation.' She tailed off; a tear trickled down her cheek, paralleling the scar. 'But no father.'

I tried to put an arm around her, I not sure why. But she stiffened again, then slowly sank against my chest. This so good. Like I protect her. My fingers drifted through her hair, 'And now, you do this.' *Damn damn damn… why I say that? So senseless,* 'So sorry, not mean. My stupid mouth again.' But I felt her smile, though not see her face. A tear fell to my chest, and a hand came to my leg, touching gently, stroking…

'Mmm,' her voice so low, so murmuring, 'the Rua sisters care for us, and about us. It was my own choice that I came to you: it has been too long since Stirior died. I was much in need when I first came to you, and I am still.' Her fingers touched at my leathers, pulling, slipping, undoing. I tried to relax and let it happen, lifting to slip out my clothes, and she was sinking lower. Her lips parted to place a kiss, and I was gasping within seconds, her hands playing a slow rhythm across my chest and groin. My own hands had their own life, to explore again within her blouse; the unbelievable smoothness of her back, the gorgeousness of her breasts, hidden for the moment. But their splendour

75

would be remembered forever in my mind. To touch with the lightest of fingertips, I was lost in the beauty of touch that over-filled me.

'Do I get another flying eyeball for this?' Showing her the three Rua marks already on my wrist – their claims to me.

She jerked away, looked up and her hand lashed across my face. So resounding. Sharp and loud. A smile took to her face, 'I know why you said that. You try to make me not care about you.'

Is she right? I think she is. 'Graleen, you must not care about me. They kill me on morrow. All koh for me then.' *Enough of this. Fear is for another day.* I touched at her body. The delight that filled me! Such wonder. I wished it could be forever. And it was. A forever that was lost in her passion and grace and wonder. Eyes closed as she pressed me back, and slid over me; mounted me, adjusting and wriggling. And swayed, rocked and writhed for an age. Both lost in such intensity as I could never find again. An age of mind-gone passion…

It was over, she was collapsed on me, breathing so hard and loud, slowing to a near-sleep, her fingers writhing into me, and I held her tight, so much the same.

*

'Ohhh, Jeemo, girl…' So slowly did I stroke her warmth and softness. She twisted a little and pulled covers over us both, to lie in perfect peace. Only her in my world.

All through the night, I focused on *Now*, and thought not of the coming daylight. I reached to touch her, for assurance, from time to time. As I felt her fingertips on me, caressing the warmth of each other's skin.

As I thought, *'Better I die in arena, not bed,'* the dawn bells chimed.

We lingered abed for a time after the sun's rays bathed over us. But eventually, I had to sit up, cold inside. *This day will happen, whether I arise by myself, or by force.* I sat up and tried to smile at Graleen beside me. But inside me, the emptiness made me feel sick, and my smile was like water. 'You sure I don't get flying eyeball?'

She laughed, 'I can't. I'm not yet a full sister. I *would* award a winged eye if I could – You've been very good for me, and therefore for the Rua. You must have been with many ladies?' Face laughing up at me from the pillow.

'What? Me? With women?' I know my face had brightened at the thought, but, 'No,' I confessed, 'I have been blessed in the joy of one lady before now, but I know nothing of what I do, or what other ladies do – or men.' Helpless in the face of her question, I shrugged. Helpless.

'Yes, Rua Li. She felt you from afar, like a needle in her head. She risked much to find you. This close, I can feel your strangeness, too.'

I knew not what I might say

'Keep yourself this way,' she told me, dressing slowly, burying her beautiful body. 'You are strong, carved from ironwood. 'And you have innocence like my daughters. Star spede.' One kiss to my cheek – I felt her softness against the hard line of a sword-scar – and she was gone.

Not ten beats later, my reverie was startled away by the sound of shuffling and rattling outside, followed by three raps on the brass-bound door, and the ceremonial call, 'Backman. The Arena awaits.'

My time's come, huh? One hard swallow, and I stepped forward and flung the door wide. So confident.

If only.

There stood my escort squad – six massive ceremonial guards in heavily embroidered brigandine jackets and over-cloaks. *Making sure I'm going, huh? Me and the Maybe Lord?*

Captains Godrun and Briand, my steel-eyed trainers. 'You have a plan?' they wanted to know.

'Yes.' I told them, as always when they so stupidly asked. 'To follow orders of Lord Rogor. Whatever he say. That is the rule, no?' *Like Fryke. I run. Over banking to setting sun.*

From then. No choice. We wended down to the dressing halls. I saw Lord Rogor the Volko was also without choice.

'Roe-Gorr the Doormat, more like.' I watched him being reminded how to behave and uphold his position, the tradition, dignity. He shook all the time he was being dressed, but whatever he was chewing seemed to help him to stay calm. *Perchance a little glassy of eye?* He looked to have no military thoughts whatsoever, and by the traditions of the contest, the captains were not allowed to take over and organise a worthy strategy of attack or defence.

The others dressing in ceremonial uniforms of the realm, and me in a traditional Backman's garb. I sank lower by the minin, *This is disaster. We all be chopped up, or burned at the stake – keep crowd warm while they have beer. If I cry enough, will they let me off?*

The preparations took their course, and swept us along, escorted by the ceremonial guard to a wagon that was decorated in gold curls and glittering stones, pennons and silver tassels. The gilding and the finery attacked my eyes, so bright and coloured and gleaming. The forids were huge, black-polished creatures with plaited manes and tails; their flank and head dressings blinding in their brilliant colouring. A new squadron of escort guards waited, with painted shields and newly-shone pike-staffs; the bannermen with finely embroidered standards and pennons. All were armed to the head-plumes. *Still making sure I don't make dash for the hills and far away, hmm?'*

We were pressed toward a set of scrollwork steps at the rear of the wagon. The Corona Lord mounted them; trembling legs barely supported him. I was eased to the steps with him, and rose to stand beside him, holding tight to the brass rail at the front. Alone – he didn't look away from straight ahead – I stood, more cold and drained than at any time.

The wagon lurched. We both gripped tightly at the rail. Across the cobbles and out the Broadway Gate we went. The inevitable awaiting us. Straight down the slight slope into the heart of Lordstown we clattered in all our splendour. I stared at the grain of the wood; the neat patterning of the forids' tails; the carved knot patterns in the metal-worked fastenings. Anything except what lay ahead. Until we reached the main avenue.

And there, all around, we were assailed by a neck-craning crowd; a few were sombre, with eyes that searched for signs of strength or weakness from Lord Rogor and his Backman. Seeing neither in our impassive stares, they cheered and waved flags; shouted good-luck wishes and tossed sprays of flowers.

This is a carnival. My first. My last. So many people. All the throng in their best mood and clothes for the festivities. Many laden down with food, seats and flagons of beer, plus a clutch of children and grannies. Others pushed handcarts brimming with whole barrels of ale and goods to sell to the celebrating crowd. We passed a stall selling Backman Bake with Rogor Relish. It seemed to be doing good business.

It'll make little or no difference to them who the Lord will be this post-noon. They want a bloodthirsty contest, a survivor-roast, then the picnic, party and pissup – as the men in the kitchens had said. A few know their necks are on the block – the ones pushing carts weighed down with their worldly valuables, ready to flee, convinced that Sandor's soldiers would be looting their way through the town before nightfall.

Mostly, I thought, they wished Temporary Lord Rogor and Pointless Backman a good death; clean but entertaining. Some burning would be good.

The noise, the colours and flying flowers, the laughing faces, the shrieks... Rogor might be accustomed to it. Not I. So much. Almost too much. I clutched the polished rail, alongside the Corona Lord, though he a hand's length shorter. I glanced. *You must have some courage to be going through with it. You could have taken poison or something. Obliged to do the right thing by the traditions.*

I looked around – The others of our combat team were bound by the same traditions, and couldn't dream of doing anything else. Two vast guards stood behind us on the wagon – the ceremonial presence, the symbol of dignified lordliness. Not as tall as I, but they looked immense in their heavy clothing and high-plumed helmets. Gleaming breast-plates and embroidered tabards caught the midday light in eye-blinding flashes.

My own leather forest garb with dull bronze bandings seemed so drab and plain. *This is all I'm worthy of?* But it was the tradition, they'd assured me as we dressed. 'Everyone will understand its significance; you are the Lord's *Backman*.'

Behind us, three similarly decorated wagons clattered, with six vividly-dressed guards, and the two captains, each with his own full-uniformed retinue. All in all, the four-wagon banner-waving procession seemed to be an exciting, crowd-pleasing sight, especially with the advance and rear-guard troops mounted on huge black forids.

Regally, our pageant wound down through the streets and avenues, little squares with old buildings, quirky designs of brick and stonework, timbered towers and rows of over-leaning homes and shops, workshops and taverns. So old. So new to me.

So slow. So far, it seemed. Working our way through the outer town towards the arena. The multitude pulled in behind us, following our parade of doom down to the festival ground known as The Arena.

 So much noise. So many clamouring people. *I'm about to die. Slashed with swords, or*

burned at a post while the crowd shriek their beer-filled delight.

Unthinking, I followed the others into the tunnel room beneath the arena's bank. 'At least I haven't shiked myself, and nor has the lord – though it smells like someone has.'

We entered the disrobing room from the outside of the arena. It was almost bare, with white stone walls like a tunnel, and a view at the opposite end directly into the arena. Once white, the walls were now crusted with stains of blood and other fluids. *Will mine be smeared there as well?*

'You wait here, until the hour.'

All well for them to say that. Someone will wave a flag, or make a trumpet note. And we would be dead.

We waited. It was not a good wait, sitting on splintered benches. I alone, becoming more and more focused on how I would die. *Will I cringe and sink, scream or beg? Will I rant and slash and fight? Must strengthen myself. Remember the Rua woman's chants – to be strong, for the good of the realm. For unity.* Miserably, I was failing to gain strength, and despaired that my great speed would ever return to me.

We're about to be bludgeoned to death, and they'll all blame me. Be dragging my carcass onto a pyre in the centre of the arena in a dozen minins. Snota should'a given me a poison pill.

Looking around, nobody was listening. Maybe I wasn't thinking aloud.

A small cohort of officials arrived from the arena side of the room. Four elderly men and a woman, 'We have to check that all is in order,' she said. 'Your combat clothing and weapons are in place, atop the motte, just beyond the entrance to the arena , *there*.' She pointed down the tunnel to where the brightness of the arena shone in green light. 'You will find out what weapons are there when you climb the hill, just outside this room, in the arena. Now, we need to confirm the names of the five members of your platform…'

'There are many rituals and formalities to be performed,' the Guardians of the Realm informed us. 'We have to make sure we know who is who, and where you should stand. It gives the crowd time to get in, settled and drunk.'

At last, after an infinity of checking and making doubly sure, the Guardians declared, 'Noon is Nigh. Combat is upon you. Disrobe and take your place at the line.'

They stared at us – Lord Rogor the Volko, the Corona Lord – yet to be crowned and almost certainly not going to be. And at me, his useless lump of a Backman. And at the four chosen guards. They set the example, casting their dress armour aside and standing nakedly erect.

Koh, so I knew it this was to be the way of it, and I followed suit, feeling weedy beside the guards. *But they're fat, flabby and sallow smooth skin, untouched by combat. 'Might be strong defence. But,* I had to smile just a mite, *my dickstaff's at least twice the size of anyone else's. In fact, I can't even see them beneath their belly-rolls.*

They stared back at my body, or wreck, as Godrun called it. 'You're all tattered and torn; sure sign of a losing fighter,' one muttered. 'You ain't with us by choice, eh, Kyre?'

'Yeah,' another agreed, 'that's why there's two-dozen unit troopers fixed specially on you, eh? Ain't going to let you run.'

'Careful, Drex, he's got more muscle than you, and he packs it into half the bulk.' I'd just been thinking the same, and managed a faint nod to the trooper who'd said it. I'd seen him around Godrun's halls – He was keen on one of the girls who brought food round.

The Maybe Lord undressed. *Preparing for his last state occasion, but he's had the guts to come and face The Challenger, maintain the tradition. Considering we'll all be dead in a few minins, we're very calm.*

We were ushered to the fore, told to stand and wait at the tunnel entrance. Pale and pinched, Lord Rogor chewed absently on his drug-cud. Standing next to me. I looked: *at least he appears to be fully in control of his body. He's not trembling like I am, and he still hasn't shiked himself. His mind's gone drifting off with the birds, though. It's sure not here… he's dull. Must still be on the soppo leaves.*

I, on the other plate, twitch like a palsy-hand. I reach down to stop one leg juddering; I sick inside. *I'm the only one who looks at all bothered – they all accept it. Put up a good display and fall fighting for the lord. Every one of us, completely planless.*

There was no escape from this: the tunnel was lined with troopers in neutral grey garb, armed with pikes and swords, 'In case of a transgression of the rules,' smiled the senior official. Behind we six-to-die were the Great House troops and their captains, purely for support before and after the contest; absolutely no interference was permitted once the signal was given.

84

The body dragaway brigade, I gazed around, wishing I had some leaves to chew and make me not care.

Naked and waiting for an aching, shaking, age, it was bright outside in the sun, but with a chill in the breeze that made me shiver more.

One of the Seniors came before us, garbed in creamy white, 'You know the rules, one of them being that I must read them out to you now… Only the weapons that you will find when you enter the arena. They will be at the top of the motte immediately outside this tunnel. With the armour you may wear. You may defend your castlette, or attack that of Lord Sandor's Troop…' He intoned on…

I knew the arena from my far-sickle visit with Godrun's daughter. I think she said far-sickle. She was not happy when I asked her about the rules, and if I could use the sticks and stones that littered the arena. 'And do we have to climb the high mound? Is the armour necessary?'

'It is if you don't want Sandor's men slicing you up at the first touch, with all your bits on display to the whole realm.' So Wisty wasn't happy. Not the first time. *Not care.*

'But we don't have to wear the armour?'

'No. You don't have to do *anything* once you're in the arena. You can run up the motte, and cower behind the little wall if that's what you want, or crawl to their motte and throw yourself on a sword or a lance – whatever the chosen weapons are.'

'Koh, I will think about it,' I told her.

'Kyre? You're thinking of escaping? Naked?'

'Not if I have no speed to help me dodge and race past the guards and the crowd. They'd be so disserpoint-something if they missed out on their Backman-roast, wouldn't they?'

'Yes.' She sounded as though she really agreed with that idea. She'll be out there somewhere in the crowd, to watch the change of lord – Rogor defeated in *Ritualla Combatta*, as the Senior insisted on saying. 'And Sandor the Gaunt will rule the Rangelands in the same gruesome way he rules the Northern Reaches now. And you'll be no help, Kyre, without your speed.'

She was right. They all are. I no use. Just make up the team as Traditional Backman. All killed. Sandor's troops fight and kill all time. Our fat softies, me and Rogor the Witless. Only me ever kill before – forced to fight troopers in camps.

Hi ho. Must do this. Stand with them. Soon dead. Not be here. Will be koh.

I order my body to stand straight, to not shake. Never like this before in fight – always happen too fast to think or be afraid. Now, is *all* wait and think.

Behind me, my four fellow pre-corpses jammed their fists together in ritual bonding, 'Tock aye *oh*!' they grunted, and again, 'Tock aye *oh! Tock aye oh!'*

The chant was picked up by the troopers of the House around them, 'Tock aye *oh! Tock aye oh!'*

Outside on the nearby banks, the crowd heard it, and joined in – 'Tock aye *oh! Tock aye oh!'*

One minin to go, the chant spreading along the raised banks of the arena, 'Tock aye *oh! Tock aye oh!'* We were beckoned to step forward, me and Lord Rogor right to the line, naked; our chanting foursome a pace behind, quietening now they could see clearly into the sunlit space ahead – most of the arena hidden by our own defensive motte. *Sandor's fighters will be lined-up just the same, craving for the battle to begin. Lean, hard fighters, every one. Accustomed to the slaughter.*

The base of our hill-mound twenty paces away, the steps leading up to the low crowning wall we were to defend. I waited, flexing my fingers, scarcely seeing the parched grass that stretched away either side of the mound. Not seeing Sandor's opposing hill, just the surrounding banks packed with masses of flags and banners, and gaudy spectators in carnival mood, hoping the change of rule would be entertaining.

'Tock aye *oh!* Tock aye *oh!*' reverberated along the banks, a cross between an incantation and a celebratory shout for more ale.

'See!' Someone pointed. 'The count's begun – three-dozen beats to go.'

I craned to see, my heart thumping, *My life so brief, being counted away. And still I know not what to do if I have no speed.* I tried to see to the top of the motte, 'What have we got up there? Swords? Broadaxes?' *I'm not putting armour on – I get killed quick and easy without the armour. Where the frugg did my fast-speed go? I need to use wet room, or will do it here. No time. Shaking too much, anyway. Need to scratch somewhere between my legs and not be anyone notice. Perhaps tonight in another life, there be another woman…*

Halfway along the right side of the arena, I could see white-clad Senior with raised arms, changing his gestures as he counted down.

'Tock aye *oh!* Tock aye *oh!*' The arena rocked with the sound.

Twelve… Eleven…

'Hey you frugging shiker!' A stab in my bare backside. A sword point, digging deep, twisting. I

87

spun, angry that anyone would choose now to spite me. It was Godrun, face grinning. Stuck sword again, at me. Into thigh. 'We watched you, you shiker. With that scar-face Rua bitch last night.'

Nine… Eight…

'You scrugg like a turd. Shiko! Did we laugh, eh, lads?' The surrounding guards were smirking and nodding.

Six… Five…

'Got the wrong hole twice, eh? Cunny like her, can't tell which way round she is, eh?'

Four… Three…

'You couldn't screw a whore in Marchtown, much less...'

Two…

I burst in fury at him, at them. Raging to kill them all. To lash into him. Tear off every head. *'The fast-speed! I have the speed!'*

One…

'Go!' Wild-eyed, Godrun was pointing, *'There!'*

I was away before his breath had ended… a swirl of wind whipping around me. I hurl myself into the bright glare. Onto the scrubby grass of the arena. Round the base of the hillock. Into the rougher grass. The timekeeper, still lowering his arm. The new wind swirled up the dust around me. A blurred multitude streaked past on the bank. Ahead – there! The patch of white rocks. The one I'd seen on my far-sickle visit. Still there. Big as my hand. Sticking up. Easy to grasp if I— Bend. Roll. Grab the chosen one. Twist my wrist. *Thus.* Unslowed. My back bleeding from the roll, I *ran. So fast.*

Six beats I count.

Two groze paces from our starting tunnel, and I fly up the high mound of the Sandor force. Not here. *Should be here on the crest – one lookout, others dressing, choosing weapons as fast as they can.*

No. Their weapons and armour await them. I leap over the low rampart. Across the earthen floor. Throw myself down their steps.

Muscular figures coming up. Naked as me. A face with a black tattoo covering his jaw. *Sandor!* White rock swung. Face explode in splintered bone and blood. Push. Falling aside. Two identical faces close behind – realising the attack was upon them. One head crack back with the rock under its chin. My fingers, rigid, drive into eyes of the next one. Rip out again. They tumble away and I am on the following man. *Same face! Scruggit! Which one's Sandor?* Blood fountains, splattering over everyone and everything. Flail at the next one. He drops back. I smash rock again. Face split away from head. Mass of red splattering over all.

The last two still on the bottom step, mouths opening. I howl on them. And through them. Stiff-fingers straight into open mouth, deep through throat, pulling me to side. My rock hand hits the last man on the chin, sideways, cracking head back. And again, another with a downward smash – blood and head-gunge splattering wide.

I crash to a skidding halt, bare feet clawing into greasy grassy earth. Spin back to the steps. *Any still living?* I rage still. Bodies still tumbling. One moves. The rock pounds down to crush his skull completely, splintering apart. Sandor the Headless.

The one without a throat is gurgling in a panic. Another without eyes is twitching, clawing at the grass. I gasping, staggering back up the steps and finish them all: bare-foot stamps on the neck… or the rock crushing the back of a head. A neck twisted. Hard. All around is red mist. Blood dripping and trickling down the steps.

What now? I was sobbing. Tense. Drained by the violence, the speed. I slowed, crouched, clutched the rock. 'Any more? *Kyre hreshki?*' All scattered, bare-arse and balls. All six. 'One's got to be Sandor himself.'

The enemy's tunnel down there. Faces shocked. Grey-coated officials; the scarlet and blacks of Sandor the Corpse. *It's over. Done.* I sank to my knees on the stone steps, rasping for breath, heart apound, my forehead sagged to the bloody steps, *Fruggit, it's done. I'm done.*

'Urfff! Ughhh!' I'm falling down and aside. Being hit. Furious blows to my shoulders and head. Roaring and shouting all around. Weapons clashing. Steel on steel. And on me. Falling down the stone steps, men in red and black, shouting, hitting. Stabbing at me. So many. Faces incensed. Can't ward off the blows and thrusts. Trying to lash back with the rock. *Need to be on my feet.* Mad tangle of red and black hammering at me with axe and sword.

Should be finished. This's wrong. Wrong. Wrong. My fury is back, my flash of speed flickering again. Struggle to rise. Lashing at them. So many. I rip at faces, jam fingers into their eyes; claw-fingers tearing at a throat. 'Yi-uck!' A sword into my thigh. Another –

shoulder. Blade slash to my hip – Frugg! I sag. Legs no strength. On my knees under them.

Seeing grey-uniformed figures as well. The neutrals. Yelling, swords swinging and thrusting. Fighting the black and red of Sandor. A falling body flattening me to the steps; another rolling across me. *Must push them off me, can't move hands… move nothing… too many bodies. No difference now… Done. Die now. Backman finish.*

Quiet now. Calm voices. Bodies being moved. Seniors speaking. 'Yes, *that* body is the Backman. Yes, it *was* within the rules. Lord Rogor can be confirmed as victor – hear the cheering?' The voices faded.

Alone. Struggling to heave bodies off me. Lift head. See Lord Rogor at the base of the steps. Dazed, disbelieving. Captains and Seniors surrounding him. The officials calling loudly to the crowd, 'The burning of the bodies in the centre of the oval will take place as soon as the remains of Sandor the Gaunt are identified for certain. His foully traitorous men will be burned at the stakes at the same time.'

A voice complaining, 'We have to entertain them until the market and fair are ready. This contest should have gone on much longer.' They drift away.

Crushed and bleeding, nobody come to me. *Still some blood chugging through me, must move. Leave here.* Force one body off my legs. Twist over. Writhe out from under it and get up to half-kneel. Exhausted. Not move more. Blood everywhere. Dark. Smell so strong. *Fryke, keeth mi toik! My head more broken than ever. Leg not stop bleeding. Kroikit!*

No-one coming to me. Rollicking Roe-gorr and the Fat Four be celebrating. On the beer. Burn Sandor's men. Give Rogor his Lord Hat.

Good. I go soon. Sword-slash on hip bleeds slower. I press it. *Nobody cares now, huh? Good. Done with me. Rest a minin. Get away from that damned Great House forever. Fryke. Much pain, like in swamp. Bakho! Blood everywhere. Can move arms and legs limbs, move neck, muscles. Nothing broken? Nowhere in death agony, just hurt everywhere. Stabbed every-fryking-where. Cheating shikes. Just need a minin and I go, escape.*

Kneeling, I look around – two grey-coats not far. Looking other way. Sunlight. Warm. Distant noise. Cheering. *Tha's it. I'm finished with. I'm free. Go and hide somewhere…*

'Well. Here you are.'

I try to look. Black silhouette. 'Goddy?'

'Yes. Me. I thought you'd run. Hoped you weren't dead.' He sound like stone.

Not can shuffle on the stone step. 'Greedy frugger; want me all for yourself, huh?'

'Oh, yes, Kyre. I told you I'd kill you. When this is over.'

'Good. Is over. You finish job now. Easy. Even for you. Here's good place.' Show him – I touch above collar bone. 'Push here. Hard. Do it good.' *Not care. See other bodies on the steps, in tunnel entrance. Grey figures checking them. If they can die, so can I. Do it.*

'Oh, my fast movement? You did good there. Indig-something, that's my trigger, eh? I so angry. Now, sword *here*. Straight down. Hard. Do it! You really watched us last night?'

'Oh yes.'

'Jealous turd,' I mock him – make him do it. 'You should have watched while I was frugging your daughter. *Skyrimos!* She squawk a lot. *Yuff!'*

His sword straight down in chest. Exact right where I say. *Feel it. No hurt. He re-grip the hilt.* 'Yeah, just do it, Godrun.'

But he's waiting. Stopped. 'You vaggard, Kyre – you never touched her, did you?'

Jeem, hurts now. Make me cough. Hurt more. 'Not once, Goddy. You not only one who frugg people about. Now shove it deeper, you bas...' Blood in mouth. Splurting out. On steps. 'I finished here. Done with realm. Unity… Rogor. *Do it.*'

I feel his hands tighten on the pommel again, 'Good riddance, you bastaro.'

'Leave it!'

What? Who interfere? Fool. Leave me.

'We'll take care of the Lord's Backman, thank you, Captain Godrun. With the Rua's apologies, tell his lordship that his Backman will be unable to attend the ceremony.'

'Frykit! Nyoio! Fin… ish me. I done here.' I try to fall forward. But blade in chest stop me. Let me die, become *Theron.* Someone kneel with me, touching. Another, a woman hold me still. 'Finish me. Kill me. Poison pill, much appreesh… thing.'

'Hold him, Ravena. Put this in his mouth.'

'Keetio, I dead.' Cool hands touching me. Resting on my head.

I hear their words – 'Strength... Rua...' The arena gratefully darkening away.

MAGGOTS AND HAIRBALLS

The hologlobe hovered closer, pipping and glowing to indicate an incoming communication. I put down the keypad I was fiddling with, powered down a couple of tell-tale screens, and turned to the waiting contact, 'Hmm?'

The hovering globe illuminated with a facial area, someone vaguely familiar. 'Hi, Cordinator Navātæn? It's Adodd here… At Aitch'O'Nine? What used to be Moddy's place?'

'Yes, hi.' Yes, I did remember him – exotic stock breeder up in the hills, him and his partner-wife, Nido. 'Of course. Ado. How're things in the rocks and stocks? Still breeding gorgraks, and skittering round the hills?'

'Sure. What else to do out here? Er, I got a tiny problem, Coordinator. Had a small space craft land on my property couple of days ago. I say "land", but it was a bit heavy coming in, probably on a damaged auto-system, by the looks of it. More than just a few dents and scrapes. In fact, it's a wreck – non-flyable – deletion job. Just making sure I'm entitled to claim it? Might be some salvageable electronics… metals…'

'Absolute. It's yours,' I told him. 'That's the second in the sector this season. Just keep me up with anything significantly new; weaponry, drive system, anything the gov might need to be aware of. Koh? But property rights are all yours.'

I could see he was hesitating…

'Couple of survivors, too, Coord,' he said. 'Don't really like to just drown'em.'

Survivors are a pain, but, morally, we have to look after them as best we can. 'What are they? More lepidos?'

'Not sure,' he said. 'They don't look much. Pathetic pallid things like little slugs with arms and legs, tangled up with each other. Hardly prise'em apart.'

'Larval form of some alien species? Whyn't you feed'em to the gorgraks? They like live meat, I gather…'

'Ah, come on, Coordinator: you're supposed to be the one who knows these things.'

That put me in my place, 'Yes, yes. You're right, Ado. Have they got chips? No? Any other readout data you've managed? No? Let's see…'

I brought the info holoscreen into being and let it attach itself to the globe. It began to fill with data, composition readings, measurements, 3Ds… 'Could they be one of these?' I spun the holo so he could see.

'Yeah, yeah – stop there. Like that one. What is it?'

I studied the info on the image, 'This's suggesting they could be ummani-kee. possibly humans. Yesss. I reckon they're humans. Hmm, first for a few years.'

'I never saw any before.'

'Nor me. There were a few out in Denya. Don't think they lasted long; seem to recall that some went wild. Others faded off. It was thought they were maggots;

intermediate form of something normal, but they seem to cease development at that stage. Maybe they need a different environment.' I flicked my arolia through the holos and data streams, quoting to him, '"Best kept singly. Problems in pairs and groups…" According to the data here, yours are less than half the weight and dimensions of the ones that were on Denya. And their chemo readings are balanced differently. Makes it seem like they're very young; hardly out the egg casings, perhaps? I imagine they're less likely to survive at that size; maybe they need yolk sacs? There's nothing about any that small previously.'

I flicked through the info-dump, 'Not known to breed… So probably larval.'

'Good. Two's more than enough.'

'Any bodies in the wreck?'

'Six, we think. Completely mashed. These two were in a pod, cocooned.'

'They looked after'em, then? Important to'em? Probably were new-hatched, shielded. Why not ask Nido if she can find any gender diff? She'll know an iskwa from an inini. Just strip their outer coverings off. Make sure they're breathing air before you do it, though.' I imagined him doing it and the pair of them gasping for breath. 'Make sure you check'em after, too.'

'I reckon my Nido can manage that. What about repatriating them?'

'Repatriate? Where to? They hurtle through here regardless, at Full Ly-Zero Speed. They cover a light year in a few dodamins or so. For them, it's like taking a non-stop hoverway trip for five days. Who looks out the windows and wonders where they are? We never really care where they're coming from or going to.'

I sighed, deflated my spirio sacs and gave Adodd a bit more attention. 'You know how it works: this's a sector that suffers occasional electro-grav storms. They can totally wipe a ship's tronix, and maybe the life in it. This's been a slow season – we sometimes get five or six derelicts. I suppose even that's not too bad, out the thousands that come through. The way markers are badly sited: they ought to be out past Suwa. That'd avoid all the traffic cutting through here – or not, as the occasional case might be.

'The trouble with trying to care for'em,' I fazed my way through the holoscreen details, 'is that we don't know what they might be like normally. Do things like these have a "normal"? Or an adult form? There's nothing here on the data banks about their natural environment. Air requirements? Not known to be carriers of any notifiable diseases, it says here. Food is whatever they have with them. There's been an ingest analysis I could let you have – see if you can concoct something?'

'I can't keep'em, Navātæn.'

'It's that or drown'em. Do what you can, hmm? Look, I'm out in your Aitch area in a couple of days – suppose I check through these analyses and see if I can get some stuff together they might eat. I'll call in, see you, koh?'

I thought he looked relieved as he logged out, and I faded the holos.

Coordinator Navātæn, huh? Is that what I am? Fat lot of coordinating I'd just done. I had a slight guilt trip about dismissing it all – a pair of possible-human flotsam – hardly of any importance, but, I briefly scoured the dumps for further info, and absorbed what I thought might be useful – humans… rare, origin uncertain, have a form of CG6-DNA. CG6 indicates common genesis with about a tenth of known space-species. Possible larval form of something larger. Recent examples… none. Language unknown. They have an inverse structure – soft exteriors, rigid structures inside. They are easily injured; don't often survive catastrophic ship events. Difficulty in self-repairs. Need the most basic training. Seem to wilt in the face of the least hardships. *Isn't that just what we need. I'll check around for anything that might be useful to Adodd. A modicum of help for them might be good publicity for us.*

Starting with Doro with her sanctuary… Nothing useful there. There's nowhere to place them with others of their kind. The small group on Terata is full – their specimens are kept singly, and the carers have enough on with that. There are too few humanic-types to know what they need; and too many for us to cope with.

I wonder… If Ado really can't cope, I'll see if Mena Gerie can take them in, at least for a time. If they're just early larvals, she might be able to house them with the other small strays and suchlike she shelters.

I buzzed through. Explained. Mena G shook her heads in chilophic wondering, 'I'll go through my memo dumps and see about them. Humans, you think?'

She was back to me before suck-time, 'No, I never had any here. What are they? Look like the maggot stage of something on the info banks? Grubs? You could try the Terata lot – they have eight or ten humans, I gather. Don't sound like they're thriving, though.'

'I already checked. Terata's above capacity now; it's only a small facility. You got anything similar you could put'em with? Some strays they might tolerate?'

Mena G fibrillated in doubt, 'Can't think of anything remotely like them. We have some things with a similar body temp, might tolerate the same environment. They were the only survivors from a come-down about five years back. Common Genesis Six? – that grouping merely means they're non-chitinous, non-crystalline and non-para-mandibular.'

'Not got much going for'em, have they? Just a heap of negative values, eh? The only apparent common factor being both lots are alive.'

'They've both got only one head. It looks like the humans have patches of hair... and my things – well, I call'em hairballs. Covered in it. Weird, they are.'

'Maybe comparing hairy patches will be enough to encourage them to get on together.'

Doro Thoscue! It was a slimepit of a tenndy – ten days fending off all the farming and forestry lobbies that were at each other's cervices...

Two building contractors suddenly interested in some low-lying land out by the west coast… New aero and space landing extension at Myriab Cusp. All needed coordinating.

With all the crises, it was a couple of tenndys before I managed to get to Aitch sector. I'd buzzed and apologised a couple of times, wailing off at the last min. *At least I sent some food trial packs I had made up from the analysis specs.*

Haven't heard back from Adodd, though. He's probably throwing a nakudu. Or lost'em already… fed'em to his gorgraks? Like I haven't got enough with all these transport breakdowns and rebuilding projects to coordinate after the floods… And Regional wanting to trial some ferro-null growth types over at Grinji.

So now, out the bloop, Bosso at Central gets an itch on his antennae and takes an interest in the ummani-kees at Aitch. An interest? Huh – "Merely a suggestion, Coordinator," he tells me. 'But if they're a pair of human kitts they might be malleable. "Perhaps more amenable to learning Chickish? See if we can settle them better than the adult specimens."

There was obviously more to it than that. They hadn't had early-stage larvae before – the group at Terata didn't breed, and nor did the singles – so they weren't Parthenos. Bosso had the idea that kitts might spark them off; and could quite possibly lead to funds to amalgamate the survivor remnants – create a viable group. Try to integrate them. And if someone at Central had an idea, who knows where it might lead? Funding, maybe?

So I went out to see Adodd, and arranged for Mena Gerie to meet us there.

The ummani-kees were squidgy little things, soft and pallid – only two eyes, single lens. Hair only on what looks like their heads. Weird creatures.

Ado and Nido had got them feeding. But some of it's the food I sent out, and we can make up plenty of that sort of thing. Bosso said Central would pay, and we should vary it to keep them interested and feeding; he'd read that on a screech somewhere. Bit of a pet mission for him, I thought. Ado had worked up some slime and scrunchy stuff that his gorgraks ate, and the ummani-kee maggots picked at that, too.

Nido had taken them on as a little project, as well, and researched about them – not exactly *researched* as much as blipping round the others who had singles, or the group at Terrata for hints. She was keeping them warm, grooming their hair patches, talking with them – apparently, they learn new words quite quickly, but they do a lot of clutching each other.

Mena Gerie arrived not long after me, and had brought six of her oddment-survivor things to see if they related to each other, or at least could be kept together. 'They breed, so I can spare a few. I say breed, but they just produce tiny copies of themselves that expand slowly.'

I looked at the cage she'd brought them in – half-a-dozen hairball things with peculiar flat-dish antennae on top that twitched at every sound. 'They don't have much in common with the ummani-kee, do they? You sure about this?'

Mena shrugged. 'Can but try, although I did put them in with some other things. They fought like fonovars, well above their weight. Had to separate'em quick. Severe injuries to both lots. There's chance of the same thing here – the human kitts don't look up to defending themselves against these spiteful little scrits.'

'Suppose we do it carefully? Let them see each other; either side of a separator panel. I'll stay. And make sure we have Ado and Nido there, too?'

It was quite haemo-warming, the way Nido went into the ummani-kee cage. More of a room, actually. She'd set it up with soft cushions, sharpening plates, hidey places, and things for them to manipulate and lie on. She'd done brilliantly, from nothing. The contrast between her perfectly rigid lines and shining colours, and their soft, slightly-repellent pallor was a sight. But she squarrelled down with them, just lying there among them. And Ado pushed a glassite screen across and let the tiny hairballs in through a back-panel.

The hairballs had leg-things as well as antennae, and looked awful. They saw the human maggots. 'Similar eye types,' Mena noticed. A couple of them slithered to the panel, opened their mouth parts. 'Doro! The teeth on that one.'

'Not huge, but so long. And sharp.' It reached forward, rigid needle-claws raking down the glassite. Eyes gone to slits.

'Fighting mode if ever I saw one,' Mena said, 'They were like that with the druyacks.'

'Maybe we should call it quits?'

'Give'em time. They might…'

The maggoty kitts roused themselves from Nido's thorax, and slid to the glassite to confront the invaders. They did the same sort of thing as the hairballs – scratching at the panel with their claws. Showing their teeth.

'That's that, then. Never mind. It was a bit of a long shot. What we going to do with'em? Can't turn'em loose – either lot.'

'Your gorgraks look perfectly capable of eating both the maggots and the hairballs. That could be a solution.'

'Central has a financial interest here – we'd best give'em a bit longer. The hairballs are slow at some things…'

'So are the kitts…'

With Nido still in there, they settled down to staring at each other through the glassite, occasionally reaching out to threaten each other, making low ominous sounds. Nido commed out, 'I think we might try moving the panel just a bit – not enough to let them get through if they want?'

So we did. Both lots were at the gap straight away, clawing at each other, making low ominous sounds – like ponkuits do when they swij-fight. They scrabbled at the glassite and they were through, at each other, all claws and screeches and susurrating.

I know my mandibles were flopping. I was sure they were going to destroy each other. 'Look at them: they're already ripping each other apart.'

'No, wait. They're not leaking. No haemolymph yet.'

'Theirs is red. None yet. Doro! Look at'em – all got their claws gripping into each other; trying to crush each other now. Better separate them quick.' But it was too late for Nido to do anything. They were rolling about, fighting. But still no haemo-leaks. They were squeaking like fornilats on the cooker.

'Still no haemo, Nido. Shall we leave them together for a while? See how it develops?' We watched them till my malpighias told me it was time for sucks and we left them to it.

Interesting place Adodd's got: those gorgraks are really awesome, and his ferintal-processing is something to behold. His nectarics are something to drool for, and we spent a long lazy midday on the sucks and crunks. I practically forgot about the ummani-maggots and the hairballs, but we went back to the accommodation eventually, not really expecting many survivors. If any.

Doro Thoscue! I have *never* seen anything like it. There was Nido spread out on her back, abdo-up, palps quivering and antennae down. I never get one of'em acting like that. And these things were all over her. Lying in a heap, eyes closed, all tangled up in each other, and in her parsilegs, and across her abdo.

Doro! It took my breath away. I had spiracles closing down. Even Nido was making that same low sound as they made, like a buzz. No haemo leakages. All very slowly stroking at each other and making the sounds, like nuzzling into each other and into Nido.

105

'Our two humanics,' Nido commed, 'are called Peter and Daisy. They've named the hairballs Jimmy, Jack and Joe; Jessica, Jemima and Jasmine.

'They told me, "They're not hairballs, Nido. They're pussy cats."'

MIRADOR

Now it ain't no use ya going on.
Yuh say I should'a reported it.
But I was in the wilds of Maine
And radios weren't around back then.

Roads? What roads? You have to ask?
They're under snow that time of year
When I came across that burned-out wreck
Far off the road and into the trees.

Like a wagon of shining metal, it was,
And smoken glass. The roof was gone,
Like the folks inside: shattered,
Grotesque and charred and black.

Seven, I count, when I pulled them out,
All blackened bones and crumbling flesh,

Though it took me a week to work up the guts
To even try, and only because *she* made me go.

'Mirador,' she said when I asked her name.
So I call her that, my rescue child, my frozen one,
Thrown clear, and broke in her arms and legs.
But her mind was sharp when she stared at me.

It was like she was reading my trains of thought
Cuz I'd looked at her in the ditch that day
And I'd thought, 'She's skinny, but who's to know
If I ravish her here and bury them all?

For a second or two, it lingered in me,
That lusting thought, but she was small
And all broke-up like mine had been,
And my lusting died and I carried her back,

Real careful-like to my backwoods shack
To strip her off, and into the bath she limply laid
And soaked and warmed and stayed alive.
And she realised as her eyes gazed round,

Filled with panic and the water thrashed.
But I kept her still and I mumbled low,
'Your arms are broke; you're dying of cold.
So just keep still and do as y' told.'

You'll never have seen the likes of that:
A full-grown man in his boots and furs,
And a girl in the bath without a stitch
'sep slats off the bed around her legs.

And I had to go slow and cautious then,
For I felt every pang the same as she.
Put into my head by her, I knew.
So gentle I was, till it came to the arm

Where the bone stuck out all shattered and raw.
And I knew she'd shriek when I pulled it straight
And bound it up. So I braced myself and got a grip
And jerked and heaved and screamed inside.

And I felt my own arm bite and grate inside
As she stared at me in challenge and hate
Till I got her out, real gentle, slow and dripping wet
And trying to smile through all the hurt.

Over the days and weeks to come
I fed her, warmed her and cherished her deep
And clothed her in my own kids' stuff:
I know they'll never be needing it now.

For they're still out there beneath the weight
Of a falling cliff that buried them all
And the cabin and horses and chickens, too.
'So it's better if you make use of them.'

Though I kiss each one before I hold
Them next to her, and I'm helping then
To put them on, like I'm saying goodbye
And denying their deaths each day since then.

Better she gets, but speaks to me
In some foreign tongue of which
I scarcely gained a word or two.

So I talked with her in English fair.

'If it's good enough for George the Third,'
I said, 'it'll do for you, my girl.'
So we healed and talked and learned to walk
And handle spoons and don our clothes.

Then came the spring of eighty-eight,
And the snows went late and sank away;
And the ground was a rug of rotting leaves
And mossy rocks and the seven graves

I'd dug and filled those four months past.
We stood by them and she held my hand,
And decided then we were ready to leave
Though I know not where I thought we'd go.

Perhaps some place where her name is known
And who she is, what tongue she spoke;
For she wouldn't say or didn't know
Just who she was or whence she came.

She learned some words and we chatted oft
And I never saw her naked again,
Though I reddened inside each time I recalled
My first foul thoughts that day we met.

'Perchance we could cross to Canada,'
I said, 'for things have changed in America
Since we broke away from Good King George
In eighty-three when a Treaty in Paris

Declared me a rebel against the crown,

And I don't want to live with that.'
So I thought I'd best face up to the split
From my family's grave at Coldbluff Bend.

Over the winter with Mirador, my shylene girl,
I'd learned to accept that they were gone
And *far away* is in the mind;
They're just as close as they always were.

So now I'm sure they'll not complain if I move away
From their landslide mass that's covered
With trees and will soon be gone from all men's sight.
And Mirador? I didn't know her mind or want.

Nor even what I myself might truly want.
Or what's allowed or where she might
Have family who miss her bright and serious smile
As we grew together and roamed the woods.

'We'll walk,' I said, as I checked my map
'To Edmundston.' And hefted the bag,
And turned my collar against the wind.
I opened the door and held my hand for her to take.

Someone was there, full eight feet tall
Blocking my way with a face from hell
And demon eyes that danced and blazed and fixed
On me. He looked to her and back to me.

Instant rage in his ghastly face I saw
And fire that burst with roaring flame
That sucked me up and scorched me through.
'Nyahhhhh!' I heard her scream in vain.

She tried to stop that fiery blast,
Though I knew that creature had come for her,
As down I fell; burned and dead and pained,
But staring up and seeing her blaze.

She's flown at him in a shrieking leap,
All hugs and squeaks and they turn away.
And I'm left alone on my timbered floor
In so much pain as I twitch and scorch.

I stole their child and they've come for her,
And in my mind they see my thoughts on that first
day,
    And I'm so ashamed, and my breath comes hard
    In harsh-felt gasps that sear inside and wrack me dead.

I know I deserve to die for what I thought
When I saw her lying there so broke near death.
I wonder in pain if Marie and the boys
And my little girls will know me still, the other side.

I'm fading dead, and voices I hear,
Close and deep and in my head. They're back,
And at my face, my Mirador and Demon Eyes
Are breathing deep and drowning me.

'Twas all so long ago it seems
Since there I laid and smoked and recovered slow.
My clothes burned through, but my body anew,
And I'm living still as I see them fade and go.

I'm at peace with myself and life and death

And Marie and the five who lie there still.
In peace *they* rest, as well as me,
Taken from me by God's own hand.

Every year I keep that day when Mirador left
And marked my birth as a man reborn,
For I've not been ill for ten score years.
Girl-friends I've had, but families, no;

And a settled foot I've never had.
I work and save, and love and leave
And keep up with things that happen around,
And something I learned two days ago:

A guy on TV who called himself an astro-phys
Philosopher, and spoke on stars and space and such.
And a universe that's parallel,
And a hole that's black and you know what he said?

'A black hole's like a mirror door, we think.
A two-way window, and door as well,
From one reality into the next.'
And then I knew what my little girl said, my Mirador.

ORBITAL SPAM

'Drew? You there still?'

I felt down myself to make sure. 'Yeah, still strapped down in Seat Two. Everything went dead. Total black. What's gone wrong, Skips?'

'No idea. I was about to declare Orbit Achieved when all systems zilped – shadow-side black.' His voice was disembodied in the sudden void.

Not even any console back-lights; no over-strip glows; no screens. 'I didn't touch anything different. I've no idea what could cause complete loss of engine power, lighting, heating, air...' I recounted the dead units around me.

'Keep your hands off the whole kittenwake till we find out what happened. Navvy systems are out, too. *Everything* is dead. We've suffered a blackout of *all* electronix. Let's stay calm. We'll get it all back. I'll grope round for the Master Override System. Something must have tripped it.'

Skips did his usual share of sighing and loud lip-sucking as he weighed it all up. 'This's bad, Drew. We need to make it less so, get some light and power back, before we can fix the engine. If it comes to the worst, there's the orbiting station we were aiming to match up with; or someone from the surface. They'll have technicians.'

'And, without any communix, we contact them how, exactly?'

An age of unseeing fumbling round the control room didn't help a lot, but we stayed calm, and talked over the possibilities of cause, and remedy. We were worryingly lacking in ideas for both.

Slowly, we gained some light from outside, the planet below reflecting through the panaviews; then actual direct sunlight. It was enough to help us locate the emergency drip-power from the battery banks, and we began to feel slightly better, finally starting to recover from the shock.

'We're both intact, Skips. We've got the lighting and heating running on low. We'll be fine.'

'Don't talk drizzle, Drew. We've had near-total loss of reserve power, certainly no ability to restart the engine. And we're in orbit round a planet we've never been to before. It don't come much deeper.'

'What the Huuk happened? We dropped out of s-drive, located the three system planets on the navvv-screens, fixed on Wertis, slotted into orbit— Total dead, just as I was readying for Systems Down Status.'

'Well, we're in the right place: that's definitely Wertis below.'

Another four hours and we had the No-Job-Too-Big's air systems linked in and half-powered. Then the outside cameras and communications at about ten percent power. We

116

broadcast a Yelp Meg, but there was no way of knowing if anyone was receiving.

'I fixed the navigation system.'

'Forget the shogging Navvy, Drew, you Cerbro Merda! We know where we are. Don't need any more than that. Get on with the manuals, fuse pads and relay-closers.'

'You said you'd do them.'

'Don't argue. Check the Dio-cut-out banks, huh?'

Hello – touch of temper there? He doesn't like me arguing – Peasy, his regular sideman wouldn't dare. He's Skips' nephew, and has to do as he's told. But this's one of our regular joint enterprises, just me and Skips as partners – him senior because it's his ship. But equal on the contracts, once we arrive on site.

'So tell me again what we're doing here, Skips, this Wertis.' I thought I'd just remind him I wasn't Peasy, and he gave me his sideways looks for a mo while we stared out the visis at the curving surface far below.

'Underdeveloped planet, fairly new colony wanting contractors to come in to undertake a range of major projects.'

'Like the water control bid *I* worked up? and the bridge project *I* designed?'

'And the road construction bid *I* did; plus the base work for a shuttle port. *I* put proposals in on half a dozen projects we could handle.'

'For us to handle *together*,' I reminded him. 'Partners, Skips.'

He grumped. 'Yeah, okay – *both* of us – invited in to take a closer look and come up with a definite scheme and price for all of them.'

We kept up the efforts to boost power on the communix, and to troubleshoot the basic cause of the all-systems failure. Semi-darkness and creeping cold were no help with the effort, or with morale. After a double-shift together, and feeling fairly desperate, we took a break and looked out – the surface of Wertis slowly exposing itself below. 'I don't see anything special about it that could have caused this bother – Type 3-b sun spectrum, habitable Type 1, temp range mid-norm; sixteen years since first survey; eighteen smallish population centres; no major towns. Six colony ships landing is all – hardly a racing start, is it?'

'Down there, see? Signs of agriculture, mining…'

'Lot of barren land, though.'

'That's why they welcomed our proposals – potentially big boosts for their developments.'

'Yeah, right, they've scarcely begun expanding away from the initial colony sites. But none of that matters, Skips, the only thing that's important now is that we're stuck. Plus the how-we-get-out bit.'

The landscape stared silently back at us. 'A little on the red-rust side for my taste,' Skips pulled a face.

'This all started as a general call-out. We got the details of what they wanted, put our job-props in, and they wanted to take them further – have a close look. Invited us in.

'There'll be a lot who simply turned up to suss it out on the spot.'

'Whatever, they broadcast the request. What did they expect?'

'Maybe too many to deal with?'

'Not us. We did it by the tenets.'

Another day's labours didn't get so much as a hum or a burp from the engine, so we stayed without the means to run the systems on full; or trigger the start-up sequence. We sent broadcasts out, but had no idea if they were being received anywhere.

'Skips! Come here. Incoming communication!'

We listened and fiddled and juggled and tuned and upped the gain, and picked up snatches. 'It's an answer to our broadcast.'

'From somewhere close by.'

Slowly building up a picture of the situation. 'Oh, shuggs. This's right down the pit-steps.'

'So. I have this right, huh?' We sat back in the gloom that used to be the control room. 'We're not the only ones incommunicado in orbit?'

'It very much sounds like there are seventeen other craft in orbit here. All dead, same as us.'

'Two humanic, eleven antopes, three from Canta and one from Godalone knows where.'

'That's about it,' Captain Xebb of the Vitro Queen told us, in a series of static-filled snatches.

'There's us and another humanic vessel, the Sir Vayer. We have limited communications with Captain Sonjer. The antopes are at the communix all the time among themselves, trying to figure it out. They managed to drift a couple together and link up, apparently. But we haven't been able to approach the Sir Vayer – we're both totally out of mains power to alter our orbit by even a degree.'

'Same here. Emergency cells and sump power only, re-routed for minimum usage.'

'It sounds like we're all here for the same reason—'

'Colony contracts on offer?'

'That's about it. We're a contractor in glass constructions. The Wertians asked us to discuss provision of ultra-glass mouldings for surface domes, quick-form repair bays, observatory globes – a hundred uses around the worlds.'

'You talk like an advert.'

'It's amazing stuff. They must have heard of us somewhere and requested samples and demos... invited us to turn up. The Sir Vayer is a colony surveyor. She inspects specific areas and makes suggestions for what could be developed there; and then produces designs for whichever proposals the customers like. Near as we can tell, the others are the same – the antopes and the trio from Canta. They antopes're furious; reckon they're going to sue for loss of time, power expenses and false contracting.'

'Not without any external communix, they aren't.'

Studying the screens, I thought I could identify a few of the other craft locked dead in the same orbit. 'The weird tracery one – I reckon it's *that* one, all lines and spaces like a net on the rad-screen. And *they'll* be the two humanics,' I touched the screen at the two dots I thought looked to have humanic-freighter size and shape signatures. 'Locked into the same orbit as us… perhaps an hour ahead.'

'Those must be the three Cantars…' I zoomed in, but the screen was fuzzy with quarter-power. 'And that will be the unknown one.' Seemingly a tangle of lines and spaces on the rad.

'And all the others will be the antopes?'

'Seems that way – all dead and wallowing in a parking orbit.'

'Skips,' I said. 'I've been pondering over this; and the nearest parallel I can think of is my electro-mail system.'

'You got nothing better to think about? Like getting us out of this?'

I ignored his sourness. 'Sometimes,' I carried on, 'you glance at an advert, or something of passing interest on reetail.xix or Gargoyle, and you get bombed-out with in-coming mail for a dozen dodecs afterwards.'

He blear-eyed in my direction, worn out after a shift inside the engine thrusters. 'Yeah, after a time, they're all the same. So?' He glugged at his beaker of tepid scuff'n brandiri.

'Is that how someone down there sees us? Maybe they're not too experienced at requesting development investors?'

'You thinking they invited too many contractors in? Got overwhelmed, ?'

'That's what I'm wondering.'

'Or maybe some just arrived uninvited?'

'Probably, and Wertis can't accommodate so many ships turning up.'

'I mean – a planet like this, hardly wealthy, is it? I bet they can't afford to employ so many crews…'

'So? What? They're making us wait? We been shunted aside? We ought to—'

'Nothing we can do, Skips. Power's off, remember? And some of the others have been here for thirty or forty days. The antopes arrived early, according to Xebb. It sounds like the three from Canta arrived together, on spec, not long after the first antopes.'

'And the Godalone one?'

I shrugged. 'The antopes and Cantars don't seem to know anything about him, except he's built like a web, with maybe-containers attached to the lines. As if by a force field. There's not been any talks with him.'

Looking out the panavis, in the shadow of Wertis, there were scattered stars everywhere. 'I'm trying to get a visual on the Vitro Queen – I think she's the next one ahead of us in the orbit. Might be that silver dot; it catches the light sometimes.'

'Could be anything. It's not like we can meet up, anyway. We're stuck right here. Locked in orbit.'

I broached my thoughts again with Skips when he didn't appear to be in too-volatile a mood after a cold hush and fries meal that he had to open manually. Hard to tell what Skips' mood is these days.

'I was thinking about electro-mail again, what I do when I'm getting inundated with offers and trials and demos—'

'Free starters, special offers, yeah. We all get them.'

'When I get too many to keep looking at the details of every one, I start to divert them – auto-dump them all in the spam folder.' I handed him another scuff'n'coff, warmish, with brandiri to the rim; might as well get it down us while we can.

'Yeah, after a time, they're all the same.' He was thinking about it. 'You reckon this's a planet doing the same thing? Advertising for various development goods and services. And when they've attracted too many, they— Shoggit! We been shunted into a park-up orbit? All of us? Even us lot who were personally invited?

'I'm thinking that way, yes. I reckon they've simply cancelled all the invitations and pre-contracts. They'll have erased the order codes and recognition signals, and progged their monitors to classify everyone who arrives broadcasting any kind of order code as unwanted.

'What? The whole planet's doing that? Advertising for various development goods and services... And when they've attracted too many, they— We're in their Spam Orbit?'

'It's what I'm thinking. And what do you do with spam?'

'Ignore it.'

'So it fills up; so you clear it out now and again; or set it on Auto-Empty every few decs.'

It was sinking in. 'Shog.'

 'Skips? One of the antope vessels – the Glitter Star – hasn't come back in view after its transit round the other side of Wertis.'

'Shoggit. If they've started clearing the spam folder, we urgently need to do something more. I'm working with Xebb and Sonjer to combine our communix power to tightcast their order code down to the ground; make the Wertians aware of us. For shogsake – they specifically invited us in. If we can get them to acknowledge one of us, then the others, we'll be okay.'

Technically, it's beyond me, but Skips and the other two managed to set up a much more powerful tightcast to the planet; only blaring their own order recognition code. It's what captains do, I suppose.

There was a response within minits.

'Shugerty! Just an auto-reply…'

'Any signal could trigger it.'

'We *need* them to recognise their own order code. They generated it; should know it.'

'Send again.'

 'Two more antopes have vanished today, didn't make it past the transit point some time during the past twenty hours.' Captain

Xebb sounded double-worried. He was probably further up the line than us.

I updated Skips. 'And the weird spider-webby one's gone, too.'

'We'll keep on out-coding. What else can we do? Ahh! – Another response. This one's different; like feeler waves tickling the antennae, as the saying goes,' Skips offered me the headset for a listen.

'I'm working with Xebb and Sonjer on another idea – to try out the exteriention multicode. We need to concentrate the triple-boosted power on one specific building. We think it's the hub for the whole planet… commercial, communications, political. There's a cargo port on the north side of it. Looks busy, too.'

We listened, and tapped in, and linked in on the power-boost, 'Looking like it might succeed – that's where their response originated. Sir Vayer is ahead of us, and it's his priority code we're tightcasting— Shug! He's gone. Sonjer's vanished. Not even his background static signature.' Skips stared at me, not believing it. 'Play it back.'

'Oh, yurghhh. She went – just a fast fade; thousandth of a second in the visuals. Probably instantaneous actually. Just like that.' We were both shocked rigid.

 'We have to keep trying. That last response wasn't simply a general auto-echo; more like a reply-query… a specific realisation.' Skips was clutching at clouds.

'But we thought that before Sonjer went into the Big Black Yonder. It didn't get us anywhere, or them. We need to doubly individualise our output signals to them.'

'Yeah, and what happens then in the spam folder? You become irritated and empty it faster than ever – You just cuss their persistence.'

'There *must* be a way. Come on, everybody – Xebb, Drew. Every problem exists to be solved.'

'That's about the most moronic thing I ever heard.' I was in no mood for idiocy. 'Which stupid kaig said that?

'Kij Morhak.'

'Right – he was the guy who got lost in the Living Maze on Ardanour – never came out, anyway. And I don't think he said that problems were actually all solved. Just that that was why they existed – like because of some pervy god setting them up just to test us.'

Skips threw me the dead eyes, like when it's share-out day and he's thinking I haven't earned my cut. 'We haven't got long. We need drastic change – nothing's worked so far; not come close.'

'We might have come close,' I protested. 'Just not hit quite the right button.'

I got the dead eyes again. 'We need something radically different – give it everything… think think think…'

'Maybe if—'

'We're on a definite loser here, Drew. We're running out of time, and I'm out of ideas.'

'I get it. Lemme think.' *Yessss… Maybe… Unless… Think it through, Drew-lad… Come on… think. Suppose we abandon the No-Job-Too-Big?*

126

Maybe we can manually winch the outgate open, seeing as the electro motors aren't working.

Then, if we can wind the lifeboat into position using the handling winches from the cargo hold... and... and... use the jack-springs to eject us – Yes, that should work; they're manual-mechanical. Given a decent-enough push out, we should get clear enough – away from this orbit. And be out this force-field, or whatever we're trapped in.

Yes... yes. If we can produce enough of a thrust outward with the jack-springs... The lifeboat has its own power source. Maybe it would come back if we're out this dead orbit. If it does, we could go for a crash descent into the atmosphere. It's not built for an atmosphere like Wertis'. Big risk... But if we... and...

If power doesn't come back on, we'd be drifting. But we'd be in a different orbit. Maybe we'd be noticed... picked up, or fired-on, I suppose. I could set the life-boat's broadcast on YelpMeg: It should have plenty of range, penetration, wide-band and volume.

Yes. Yipps – I feel better already – might just work. Sight better chance than wallowing here. Right, let's get this into motion while I still have the procedures in my mind. Could be our turn anytime soon...

'Skips?' I came out of my deep-thought reverie, 'I have a cunning pla—'

OUT OF PHASE

'It's you who's out of phase, Yanni, not that stupid machine in Physics 501. Quantum assholes – it's *you* that's flickering, not Doc Moron's gadget.' So they're all staring at me, and knowing that Lorli Hildegard isn't best pleased with me any more.

'I saw you in class, out the corner of my eye, and you was like glimmering like a fluorescent light when it's de-gassing.' There she stands, once the love of the semester, now all lipstick and pout.

So they're all squinting at me with their eyes slit and taking a rise out of us both – her as much as me. Who cares, anyway? It's months since I was lap-dogging round after Lorli – till I found she was posting things on YoonMe and had developed a strong thing with Mgmbu Gnoi the hockey jock while I was locked away for the pre-exam swat. It was all postings like – well, I can't say, but it was all the derogatories about me, and the plaudits about Hockey Jockey Peabrain.

And my best effort at a reply was, 'What a frigging freak you are, Lorli-brain Fireguard.' That was about the most ridiculous speech I could ever of said, even I knew that, before I'd finished. But what the heck.

'Ain't nobody can get out of phase, Lorli Hildegard,' the neutrals and the stirrers were jipping at her. 'It was a waveform class…'

'It was your eyelashes that was fluttering.'

'You're just making it up, same as ever-time.'

'As if anyone could be out of phase, 'cept you and Jock the Strap.'

'Yeah, Not like sea waves and radio waves and music and stuff like that.' Andy Dieppe was on my side, 'Y'only saying it because Yanni ain't interested in ya no more.' Which I wasn't – I turned her down for a Rats Party at the weekend. She's trouble, and a huge waste of time. And I'm not going down that track again.

'You're out of phase with her,' my buddies said – and offered to show me how it's done, with her.

'Yeah, yuh definitely out of phase if you're not gonna take her up on an offer like the one she made – she's *Hot*, man.'

Her friends, of course, sided with her, even Maggi Phillipps, who reckons to be my study buddy and home-friend. 'She's got you there, Yan. You're absolutely out of phase if y' not liking the girls. Preferring study, huh? How weird is that, huh?' They always do a lot of "huh?"ing when they're in a mood like that.

It would of all settled down – the usual two-day jibe-stint. Except Lorli kept on about it – tunnel-minded creature that she is. For like – days. 'He was flickering. I saw him. I watched him. Definitely got a sort of shimmer, like he was only half here.'

And some of the others, I could feel them looking at me kinda funny in classes. Like they were checking for themselves. And it started up again, slow at first, 'You're a freak, Freako,' I was getting told at every

130

lesson break. It was her slutty crew said that, all aboard the good ship, "Screw Me Quick".

So it was on my mind a bit, and got me thinking about it... *Can a person be out of phase? Like my inner electrics aren't in harmony?* I felt perfectly normal.

I asked Teacher, and she was saying, 'They've done some voltage variations experiments with animals and embryos.'

'And they made things grow differently? Behave differently?'

'Just cells, mostly, in plants and worms. And recently with bodily organs and things. Not any complete organisms like rats or puppies.'

'Can it happen naturally? Would it change somebody?

She sort of laughed and shrugged all in one. 'I don't know if any work's been carried out on humans. MIT, Harvard, NEIT... Google it. See what there is online. You could try writing them...

Now, I wasn't gonna shock myself with 110 volts or ten thousand or whatever. I mean, it ain't long since 12 volts off my dad's car battery blew me across the drive and I got burns on both hands and I reeked of singed hair for a week. So, just out of interest, I looked into it as a 10th grade science project. And, of course, a person must have all their electrics in harmony, but it's easy to interfere with them, overpower them.

'That's because muscles and power-socket electricity happen to be the same frequency as each other,' I was discussing with Teach. 'But mains electric is a million times stronger, so it wins every time.'

'That's what "overpower" literally means, Yanny,' Teach said. 'But, get the interfering waves tiny enough, like detailed, and maybe you could make changes.'

'I can't,' I said. 'But I been looking it up, and the guys at Tufts and the Max Planck Institute have been doing stuff on transmembrane potential and finding all sorts of weird things.'

'Transmembrane? Inside people? Go for it, Yanni, look'em up.'

Yeah, Teach was alright. So I found out some more about it on Planck Ahead and Wikipedia. And booked some time in T4 Phys Lab, and the technician showed me how to set the monitoring equipment on myself and a couple of the guys, for comparison.

And I found it's all true enough – you can detect all these harmonic waves doing things across the body – every fibre, muscle, blood and brain cell. So I tried mapping some of it out, and couldn't get anything like they were getting with all their fancy apparatus at Max Planck and Tufts.

The big obvious thing was – the readings on me were so different than those on Henry and Wal. So I re-worked them, recalibrated the apparatus, got Techno Travis in T4 to check my settings, and re-did the tests. Same again. Their readings were identical, and so were Travis'. Mine were skewed.

'Don't look anything like,' Travis agreed.

'Always said you were a weirdo,' said Wal.

Henry looked at me a bit suspiciously, but he was just messing.

That was okay. My project was fine at that. I slanted it to be an investigation into the vagaries and variations inherent in measuring things – which in itself is a biggy in quantum physics. I didn't need to kill myself or Henry and Wal, with all that wiring on us any more. My results needed to be explained in terms of equipment-to-individual-subject tailoring, not simply assuming the subject is way out past Saturn in his brain and body pattern.

The Lorli-inspired sniping died down, of course and we all got on with things. I re-checked my readings and results and refined them up for the entry in the Science Project, and expanded on them a bit. I dated Jenny-Lou from Alabam'. Went to a coupla games with her – Thunderbirds on the ice, and Sting on the basketball court. And built up my credits on European History, which I was minoring in.

Some outside prof looked over all our physics projects. He was at MIT and head of some faculty that wasn't physics. He made a few extra comments at the end of mine. Wrote it was, "Well more than adequate… An interesting and original premise and good methodology… Yielding at-variance results that should be re-checked more thoroughly before final submission."

I checked the results, then replicated them. Got the same readings for me, Wal and a reluctant Henry; plus Maggi and Jenni-Lou agreed to be read as well.

Again, theirs were all very much the same; certainly solidly within "normal" parameters; but mine even further outside the standard deviation than they'd been the first time. 'Now that's a bit of a mind-bender.' It did – it absolutely shocked me. 'There really is something a shade off-synchrony about my internals.'

So I was stupid, and went and asked Lorli what she actually meant when she said that about "out of phase" that first time. Of course, she made an enormous fuss about it, mouth and boobs all a-quiver, and said, 'When I was like looking at the teacher, but could see you on my left, you was like flickering – like a neon light that's starting to go. You're a visual vibration.' She probably peed herself, she was laughing that much.

So I was more stupid and emailed the prof guy and asked if it was possible for someone's internal electro-system to be so different than the standard; and I sent him my newly expanded and verified results.

He was interested enough to reply. 'No.'

But coupla weeks later I get an email from a Post-grad guy in a research place at Tufts, Mass, saying the prof guy had mentioned it, and sent it on to them. He was interested, as my methodology seemed sound. 'Like to check out your findings,' he texted me. 'I'm doing a PhD in aspects of the physical roots of psychological structures.' Whatever one of them was.

After a couple more texchanges, it was him who got stupid, and invited me over there for a day to do some "elimination tests". Me! *At Tufts!* – like MIT, but up-market. A day to get there and find somewhere to stay. Had to be cheap – I'm on a scholarship budget.

It was amazing! I had a day in this laboratory-lounge kinda place *at Tufts!,* wired up to all kinds of gear with monitors, screens and wiggle-graphs. Plus half a dozen folk plugging at me and umm-ing and er-ing and muttering and adjusting. And, like being all so dead serious. And setting up some ultra-fast cameras. And later getting a coupla other prof-types in, too. Not much of a line in chatter, though – hardly a word in any social sense – not even a first name from any of them. They were all Doc or Prof or even some student-type rank – Fellow and things like that. *Real* serious.

So then they wanted me to stay another day for more tests and talking, but I was out of funds and my bus ticket back home wasn't transferable. So somebody said I could room-mate with him, meals included. That was a bonus; and they'd make sure I got home okay.

That next day went a bit different. They had some other people they brought in from upstairs. Coupla real prim and starchy ladies with glasses – one heavy black-rims and the other thin wire. A different slant on the questions, too. Like, 'Where were you born?'

'Where do your parents come from?'

'How long have you lived in Springfield?'

'Where before that?'

'Ever been Out West?'

'What? Like Area 51?' I asked, trying a bit of levity with'em.

'Something like that,' they seemed to be saying. One of'em actually did say it. She sort of laughed, though. And they were finding it increasingly fascinating that I had no idea who my parents were. Or where I was born. It sure wasn't what I thought they'd be looking into.

'My birthday's May 4th, because that was when I was found at a maternity unit somewhere in New Mexico.'

'Out West?'

'Yeah, right. New Mexico's always been "Out West", as far as I'm aware. Come on, it must be a thousand miles across two states, with a tiny little Area 51 lost somewhere in the middle to the desert.' They were getting on my toes with this totality of stupid. 'I ain't no alien,' I said.

But it got them to thinking along even more weirdo tracks. Me, too. I was never adopted, though three couples looked after me long term. I was sort of passed on down the line and was in a social home by the time I was migrated to New England and the cold weather at Springfield. May 4th was a laugh for these guys, apparently – 'May the 4th be with you,' a couple of them joked, and another one said it wasn't no laughing matter.

They were digging, and questioning more and more, for memories and impressions, like round Farmington and Kayenta. And I was putting all this together from what they asked. The questions were in bunches: two personal queries per group of questions.

Now. Whatever anybody thinks, I'm not thick. Yeah, with girls, maybe I am. But, on the way back to Springfield Hall that night, I had a coupla hours to figure on a few possibilities: One: maybe they weren't all that bothered, after all. Decided I was a false alley or something. Because all-of-a-sudden they practically couldn't get rid of me quick enough; and the extra-extra night accommodation never materialised. So I found myself on the late-night Greyhound down the I-90 back to my cosy, tiny, cold little room. They said it was because it was the weekend coming up and the

Tufts campus was closed for some conference or something.

'We're gonna be taken up with that. We'll get round to analysing all these results come Monday.'

'Next week sometime, anyway.' So I was put in my place – seat 31, next to some gruesome kid who went to sleep on me.

Two: perhaps they'd been following some thoughts that came to nothing. Like where I was from. But they never said anything about contacting the Hall for my history. And they didn't ask about getting my DNA to narrow down what my heritage might be, my origins. Cos that part of Out West is a lot of Navajo and Ute people, Mexicans, all sorts. They could of taken swabs and samples in all their prodding and poking, for all I was aware, anyway. So they'd decided I was a dead end, whatever they'd been wondering, and ditched me, rather than spend a few dollars putting me up for another night. 'No wonder you can afford all that fancy equipment,' I said, on the way out, 'with the savings you're making on not putting folks up when you said you would.

Three: they maybe had no idea what they were thinking about, anyway. Sure, they did all the tests the first day and nodded and discussed and wrote things down and looked at me funny. And seemed to be agreeing that my own tests were, "crude, but basically correct in outline.' Assholes. They didn't mention them again. Didn't say anything to me about what it might mean. But I don't reckon it can be all that common – unless they decided it was poor readings that didn't mean nothing – like I'd half-concluded in my Project.

137

That seemed most likely, going down the I-90 with this kid dribbling down me.

Four: they had no idea whatsoever. They gave up because they didn't have no explanation for why my electro-transmembrane readings, electro-magnetic field pulse-resonance and all that, was a tad different than theirs. Thus: sweep me out with the trash. I minded a bit, because they'd wasted my time. And my time's as valuable as theirs. Boston was okay, though, what bit of it I saw.

Five: not for the first time, I was wondering about who I am. I'd always just thought I was some poor-folks' kid in Albuquerque or somewhere that direction. Maybe some young woman who wasn't married, needed to work, no feller, and all that. But now, it was making me wonder about the parents who'd looked after me. Their names; what they said about me, or about themselves – almost nothing. The changes in foster-type parents, and the places we lived. I still don't know some of the places, not even their names. Like Fayetteville we lived in at one time, but which one? There's a dozen or more Fayettevilles in the US. Same with Fredericksburg. Why were we always moving? Yeah, I know – lots of people do, but I'm not eighteen years old yet, and I been everywhere.

Six: I never thought there was this much to think on, like the questions they spent today asking and dismissing. I grouped'em. And, thinking about them, I wonder what they were imagining when they were asking. Using my massive brain – ha ha – I decided that at first they wondered *what* I am – like I'm some variety of electric alien. But they must of decided I'm no different, after all, and dumped me on this bus.

Or... maybe they didn't like what they decided, and dumped me on this bus – sweeping under the Greyhound carpet. They gave me a "Wearable Health Device" made by Medtronics, for the faculty to use back in Springfield. 'It's a body electron scanner,' Wire-rims told me. 'The heavy bit is the Base Monitor Unit. The wearable part is around half a pound.' She made it sound like Semtex. 'Don't let the bag out your sight till you get back. It cost a fortune.' So I pushed it under my seat.

Just great, ain'it? When you're wanting to get back before lockup time, Greyhound MS 124 had to wait at the Sturbridge Depot for a connection to come in from somewhere out Albany way. That was going to make us an hour late getting in at Springfield Terminal. Most folks climbed off and went to the bathroom and either went back aboard to catch up on some shut-eye, or hung around smoking.

We had plenty of time for a coffee, and I wasn't feeling sleepy, so – anything to get dribble-gob kid off me – I went in the diner and kept one eye on the coach the other side of the gas pumps for when the driver returned from wherever.

I'm sitting there, half-leaning against the cement pillar, wondering if I'd of been better off staying aboard, and not having a dull dull dull desultory conversation with this old guy who thinks a discussion is him doing all the telling. 'What y' got to realise, young fell—'

'Yi!!!' His face is shredded red. Massive window shattered right through him. Wall panel gone. I'm half behind the cement pillar one second, then flying and rolling. Glass blasting everywhere. Wall came in. Glass right through him. Instant blood. Whole diner lit up. Then blew it wide open. Like a follow-up fireball through the whole place. I'm hurtling across the floor in all this glass and tables, and got smashed into the counter and the mirrors. I'm really hurting everywhere. Can't breathe. And deaf. Trying to sit up and see. Too dark – flames flickering red is all. Feel like I'm bleeding from loads of places.

I'm crawling round and saying, 'What the... You okay? Shit, man... There wasn't enough of him left to feel anything but extremely dead. Fuckit I hurt.' But I could still move, and not many others could – There was a leg with a woman's black-and-glitter shoe. I'd seen her near the door.

Just about managed to stand up. The bar was mostly gone. Outside, the coach was a black chassis and bits of the ends. On fire., the seats that were left. Nobody alive on that.

Whummmpppp! Gas pump blew, another air-sucking fireball, roiling up in the black. Flames gushing out the ground as well. No movement at all out there... Yeah, maybe... Couple of silhouettes stumbling back.

It was jumping about in my head – *Boston... Marathon bomber. Terrorists. What if? Going for an easy target? Somebody special on the coach?*

My head's all in a twist and shock and zonking about, thinking, *No... can't be... Not me? The way they'd been at Tufts. It was a definite bomb. I didn't know what was actually in the bag they gave me – something heavy, for sure. Can't have been aimed at me. Must'a been. Can't be. Stupid.*

Just the same, I went out the back way – there wasn't really a back left. Or a front – it was still all fire that way. Real hard to stagger at first, but I'm thinking I gotta be as far away as possible, fast as I can. Real struggle across a derelict plot and into a cornfield – Deep and dark, that was, but it got me to a back road. So stupid to think it was somebody at the research labs trying to kill me. *Me!? What the fuck for?*

I hid for three days, got cleaned up and stole some clothes from a Goodwill shop. Ate at Feeding America stands and queued with all the unemployed at the Food for Life places, and hitch-hiked down to New Haven. Saw a newspaper on the street stall there, "Greyhound Bombing – Suspect Named". And it was my picture! My name and address and murky vague history – no birth registered; movements as yet untracked for the past seventeen years... *What the sluice-gates are they doing to me? Not known if I was a suicide bomber or had escaped... Remains of over thirty people still being ID'd...*

If I was older, I would of grown a beard or something. But in the meantime, a hoodie would have to do. It didn't fit that guy, anyway.

So then, I was hitching down to New York... then Philly, and it's Atlanta next. Maybe I should double up north to Chicago to put'em off my scent, and then through the Mid-West, and go back Out West. I vaguely recall liking New Mex and Utah when I was a kid. Lot of long-distance traffic going that way. No trouble getting lifts...

So. Seven: which I was getting round to before I got muttoned by the explosion. What are they afraid I am? Their questions seemed to wonder if I'm an alien who was laid here, like an egg; or perhaps implanted in some poor woman. Or maybe I was stranded when my space-ship passed through; or crash-landed, and got alien accomplices to foster me? One question-set was about parallel universes and what did I know about them? And heaps of technical data questions that I'd need to be a Nobel physicist to understand, not your average universe-hopper.

It would be interesting if I was something like that – an alien or parallel-worlder come visiting, or getting lost. I could imagine that my DNA would be amazingly different, and my electro-micro-measurements, too. *Maybe they really did get my DNA – simply collected it off a cup or a door handle?*

Then there were the questions about AI. Artificial Intelligence. Me! How did I learn? What did I feel? Had I had sex?

'Are we counting Lorli under that banner?' I asked'em.

Mostly the same as the other groups – just leaning a bit towards "Where do you plug yourself in?"

Maybe I'm a hybrid, I'm thinking. *A sport – a natural freak – a genetic offshoot who happens to have survived? Or had my parents stolen uranium and massaged their privates with it?*

So – my transmembrane electro readings had given them the idea that I was very different. Something had scared the shit out of them: they'd killed forty-eight people at the Greyhound depot – on the coach and around the filling station and diner. Man, they were scared. Police were still saying they didn't know if I'd vaporized or gone AWOL, but they were checking movements out the area that night.

I sure don't know. Am I an alien from the far side of Andromeda? Or a strandee from Parallel Universe nine trillion and one, popped out the nearest black hole? Or was I brought up in a test tube and Petri dish in Albuquerque? My money's currently on the theory that random cosmic rays affected my parents' genes, and I'm a one-off mutant.

How can I find out? Is my thinking different than anyone else's? Do I feel unlike others? Should I? If so much of me is the same, I can't be from the planet Zog. And if I don't know myself, what difference does it make? Why would they attempt to kill me? At such a terrible cost to others?

So Chicago wasn't anything like as bad as I'd imagined, and it's a thousand miles from Boston. Had a day or two there, then hitched out another five hundred miles west, and started bussing tables in a diner on the Topeka side of Kansas City.

I'm plenty far enough from Massachusetts, I figure, to rest up awhile. Getting paid in meals and night-bunk, and a few dollars extra plus tips. Here, I can stay low and catch up on the TV. They didn't have no clues about the reasons for the bombing, or if I'd escaped or died. But, anyway, this's Mid-West, and there's not a lot of interest in East-Coast goings-on. But I hate the way they flash my mugshot up on the screen now and again. I'm kinda hoping the triple dose of Trump-style fake tan changed my looks okay, but I'm still wary as shit and watching everybody, and sizing up the best trucks to hitch a lift further West on. *Give it a coupla weeks here. Let it die down…*

143

Someone must be very frightened, I'm thinking, as I'm taking the dishes over to a couple of truckers and clearing the tables near the doors. *For them to be so coordinated, so swift in trying to kill me. Some nerve they got, getting me to carry my own bomb. And desperate enough to be willing to kill loads more. Not to take chances on keeping me. Even locked away, like they surely could of done.*

Wherein lies their judgement of my humanity, artificiality or alien-ness? In an over-sensitive voltmeter? I was getting all indignant and philosophical about it by then, and telling myself to calm down, and I'll be okay. The face cuts are healing okay, I'm not limping so much now…

These two trucking guys are giving me funny looks, and talking about me. Something about the TV.

Are there some huge implications to being a fraction of a wavelength different? Does it make me inhuman? Too dangerous to humanity? Uncontrollable? Unknowable?

I *really* don't like the way these truckers're deciding something. One's got his cellphone out and studying at me and muttering, and I'm staring at him and wishing he wouldn't do it.

I'm giving him the hard warning look like they do on the movies, and sure enough, after like, five seconds max, he looks worried. Puts his cell down and he's choking a bit. His buddy's wincing and feeling at his chest, starting to gasp the same…

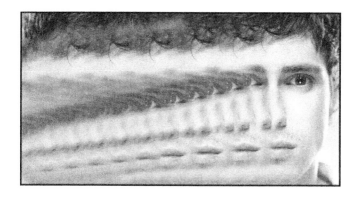

PONDKEEPER

'You know, Freddy, a really weird thought crossed my mind yesterday.'

'Oh?' He drained his drink; he was never interested in my weird imaginings. Freddy only came into my garden so he could sit in the late afternoon sun and watch the birds round the pond, while we sip shandies before starting on the vino after six.

I was out here when I first had this thought: *the pond was big enough the way I built it, years ago. But it's expanding on its own – getting more than a tad overgrown all round, especially on the far side where the rockery slumped in.*

This past couple of years, the rushes have spread well beyond the supposed edge on the far side, and the shallows extend as far into the garden as the pond is wide – it's about doubled its width. There was a heron going after minnows the other day, where it used to be the meadow-grass lawn.

'Yes,' I carried on. 'Really funny thought I had. You know them spacecraft, the Voyagers and New Horizons?' I make him listen to my astronomy ramblings as the price of free drink.

'Not intimately. Didn't they shoot off years ago, "Boldly gone to the far reaches of the Solar System and beyond" as they say?'

'They're the ones, and lots of others, like the Pioneer ones. Grand Tours of the outer planets, they called them. Landing on a comet... and a bonus fly-past with some lump of rock a trillion whatnots past Pluto – called Ultima Thule.'

Freddy shrugged and looked pointedly at his newly-drained glass. 'That the one shaped like a snowman, was it?'

'Yes, way out in the Kuiper Belt—'

'Whatever one of them is.' Freddy knew more than he pretended – for years he'd been putting up with my stories about Martians, Moonmen and unexplained signals and light bursts. 'What about'em?'

'Every single one of those spacecraft suddenly ceased broadcasting six days ago.'

'Ahh, poor things,' he was taking the piss. 'Sulking, I expect.'

'Calculating back from when their last signals arrived on Earth,' I carried on, 'and how far away they were, it's clear they all stopped simultaneously, regardless of how far away they were, or how long they had been traveling. I wondered why they all stopped at the exact same time. Why then? *That's just too weird,* I thought. *Why all at once?'*

Freddy was a bit dismissive, reaching for the bottle, 'Could be lots of reasons. They maybe reached their sell-by date… sell-by distance?'

'No. Can't be either of them,' I said. 'Something affected them all at the identical moment.'

148

'Batteries not charging up if the solar panels get dust on them? Or the sun too faint to charge the cells? Talking of which, it's getting chilly early, innit? Moon'll be up soon. We going inside?'

'Nothing like that could possibly make them all go off-air at precisely the same time, hundreds of millions of miles apart. That's impossible.'

'If it did happen, then it isn't impossible.' He grinned like he'd just come up with the definitive answer to life, the universe, everything. That did have some logic, though, I had to admit. 'You're thinking someone switched them all off? Don't be daft, George. Nobody could do that.'

'Not some*one* – some*thing*. Listen Freddy. What gave me the thought was – I was looking at my pond: all overgrown – fish among the rushes where the meadow grass used to be; frogs and newts everywhere; dragonflies and midges all over the garden – getting to be a nuisance. Shouldn't be all over the place. The pond is where they're supposed to be. They should stay there.' I nodded to confirm my mantra, studied my drink and thought, *Yes, it is getting chilly early tonight.*

'You wouldn't know it, but every now and again I do a tidy-up. Me and my Ruthie were saying yesterday about where the bank's slumping in... bulrushes, water buttercups and stuff spreading way too far.

'She's bored over the summer holidays, so she fancies making a big project of it. Rebuild the sides with the rockery stones, and reset all the paving slabs

149

this side, and make it real neat, like it used to be. Root all the bulrushes out, get a ton of soil to refill that sunken area and grass it over. Keep all the plants and frogs where they're supposed to be.'

'So?'

'I was thinking how it's a parallel situation with these long-distance space-craft. It's as if something doesn't want us to leave the solar system. It's pondkeeping us; putting barriers up. Making us stay here, within its limits, tidying up round the edge.

'Course it is,' he said, waving his glass at me. 'You gonna put a drop more in this?'

I ignored him. 'Think of another reason why they should all cease operations in unison.'

He shrugged and again stared longingly at his empty glass. 'You tell me; you're the pondkeeper-astronomer.'

'No. *He* is. Up there. Like me with my pond, I reckon the Big Pondkeeper up in the Sky had a look and realised his edges had crumbled a bit, and we were spreading too far, and now he's reinforcing his boundaries. Getting rid of anything that's strayed too far.

'He'd just chuck stuff back in.'

'No. Think about it, Freddy: usually when I do this pond, I clear out the excess lilies and weed, and suck some of the mud out the bottom. Maybe cull a few of the excess fish numbers – down the reservoir. I might leave a hose on overnight to flush some of the stale water out. Give it a fresh start.'

'Ne' mind all that, George. It's definitely getting a bit of a chill now the sun's gone. Let's go inside.'

'In a minute. It's just like it is with The Big Guy Upstairs. You know how many mass extinctions the Earth's had? At least five. Desert world… comet collision… giant asteroid? Continents merging to form Pangaea? Every time, different species wiped out. He's doing exactly the same with us as I do with the pond.'

'Yeah, right, so your pondkeeper doesn't like dinosaurs, eh?'

'Or thousands of species that were wiped out after the Devonian, and the Permian. Perhaps somebody up there's getting impatient with evolution? Maybe our pondkeeper decides to specialise in something different now and again, clear some of the old stuff out, try something new, or make things easier for one particular favourite – like birds, or mammals. Or dinosaurs, like you said yourself.'

'So Iceball Earth was just freshening us up a tad, huh? They're all natural… cosmic accidents…'

'That's probably what the fish in my pond think, too. My Ruthie was helping me to clear some of the big lilies out yesterday. Suddenly, she says if we're going to all that effort, then we might as well do a proper job; and try something completely different.

'So what's she got in mind?'

'Laugh all you like, but she tossed a load of food in yesterday so they could have one last happy feast. And told the fish she's going to clear them all out, and all the plants, too. And the mud and everything. She'll do it, alright – she's very determined when she gets started – look how she did all the decorating last year. She had a sudden yen for a neatly-trimmed lawn for the kids to play on, instead of a vermin-infested swamp, as she refers to it. All the goldfish and shubunkins'll go to GardenLand Aquatics; the crayfish, frogs and newts'll be in the Erewash canal; and the weeds to the council tip at Giltbrook.

'Then she'll flush it all out with the pressure hoses, and refill it overnight. She's seen koi carp on the net. Wants some silver and gold-glittery ones from Israel. They'll need extra-clean water, so she's been online shopping for a big filter and UV system, water circulator... bubbles pump. Special foods — whatever it takes, she'll get it set up within the week. It's the way she goes at things, once she's decided. She'll be tired of it in a couple of years. It'll go downhill, the frogs'll be back, the dragonflies, and it'll all start again. Just like the Earth.'

Freddy was looking around, pretending to be worried, 'There's going to be some sign of a universal hosepipe bearing down on the solar system?'

'Just the Earth. Think in terms of an ultra-massive solar flare,' I said. 'Or a comet gone astray. A wandering black hole or supernovae next door? One of Jupiter's moons getting nudged this way?'

He was gazing up again; the moon had risen over the trees, and the low clouds had drifted away. He looked a mite puzzled. 'George?' he said, 'Have you ever seen the moon looking *quite* so enormous before?'

PRASAP1

The pyng-tuus are still twittering on their perch; they're like Space-force majors on a bottle a day. My kids keep tossing fickle nuts for them to feast on, so they'll carry on with their antics while the supply lasts. Hi ho – Happy Days, huh? Kids and pets – if it's not one lot, it's the other.

An ii-message pops up on my screen. I don't think I've ever received one that made me jump like this one. I mean, it isn't a horrible picture, or a shrieking cartoon, or anything the kids are always sending to each other. It's simply a few words.

"Are you the Mary Hill from Pentekky AstroPort 7-9? Prasap1"

I don't know why it shocks me quite so much. Yes, I do. *Pentekky!* So long buried. Coming up like a bony hand clutching at me from a grave. A voice echoing from my darkest past. I'm shaking. Hollow. I can hear the echoes within. Shocked. Wondering – *Who in the Pit is still alive from those ghastly days?*

Prasap1 – Please reply as soon as possible – One minin. That's common: it requires your immediate response, before you've had time to research it, or think up a clever reply.

"Yes", I button back in auto-reaction. And watch the spectrum screen swirl to a point as my reply takes flight. *It can't be anyone who was there. Everyone from Pentekky 7-9 died.* I'm suddenly re-filled with memories and fears of that time. Welling up inside me.

Awful times. Eight years ago now. It seems so far away. That winter with *Him*.

"Prove it." The screen challenged me with its new message a moment later.

"I know who I am," I tapped. "Who are you?" Some silly time-wasting advertising scammer, no doubt. My finger hovered over the Foff key.

It bipped back. "Moppy?".

Moppy? *Moppy?* Once *my* name. Only one person, ever, called me that.

Automatically, I'm sending back. "Bouncy?". I gaze around my *huone* apartment, recalling the rags and slime and broken concrete we were surrounded by back then. A lifetime removed from the ultrene-patterned walls I have now.

It's impossible. Someone being stupid, malicious. Bouncy was killed. He vanished as the war was finishing. Captured by the Qinting, it was said, when they hit with that overwhelming counter-attack – all glittering eyes, weapons and uniforms. Ambushed in the rubbled streets and cellars at Pentekky. No-one who went to Gareki Square survived that fight. Such a desperate day it was, with the city ablaze. Perhaps twenty of our people were lost on what turned out to be the last full-fighting day. *He* never came bouncing back again.

Afterwards, there were different tales for each of them... "Oh, I heard Jimmy was lectro'd... No, it was Peets: he always had the sonic guns. Aldin was found dead with radiation burns a few days later. Matry died with that blonde lad... *he* was a girl – not that anyone could tell – so many bodies were charred so badly in the fires. Mikl was definitely captured – they zioruptured his brain. Was it Mopes who caught the blue plague? No, that was Yessi. Three buried in the rubble were never identified – so long afterwards when they were found."

I never cried for *him* and his awesome eyes. I should have done. But there were too many who disappeared before that time. And still carried on dying afterwards – of the winter's cold, or wounds, infections, starvation, the fire and gas attacks when the Qinting came through. There was always so much to be done for the living. No time or spare emotion for crippling regrets, or times to yearn for.

I still don't know who won the war – us or the Qinting. I doubt anyone knows. Everything petered out. The world calmed. The Conflict slowed in a series of nobody's-attacked days, agreements and truces, so the rumours said. Our cell wasn't receiving supplies; connections to medic facilities were broken; refugees no longer flooded past; we heard of repair and clear-up squads. A time of hatred and dragging strife, and total uncertainty about everything. Cold, grey world.

Eventually, we began to see Qinting in all sorts of places, with their facet eyes and flexi-limbs. Always in company with our people at first, so not exactly integrating, or merging; being escorted round, but clearly cooperating in offices, stores and some rebuilding projects. It was traitorous to collaborate with them – or them with us – after everything we fought for.

No victory. No defeat. No pronouncements. Our world simply re-settled, and sank, and became pointless.

I remained in the cellars for ages. There was nowhere else to go; the surface was blasted and poisoned as far distant as anyone knew of. So we stayed in the communa. We worked on the fire-wrecked buildings, and were paid in tokens, or scraps to eat, or clothing. And we grieved, and accepted the status quo, whatever it was. And rat-struggled for existence. The few of us who were left alive. Fewer still by the time the summer came and went, and we were into another cellar winter beneath the deep snows of Pentekky.

Of course, things changed. We came up to the surface for longer periods, and stayed there after a time. It became better than it had been through all the years of fighting. The freedoms weren't the same, but some improved and increased. We're comfortable now, and we've seen Qinting in most suburbs. They aren't in charge, so we didn't lose. Just living and mixing. It's more as though the war drifted past us, faded off somewhere else, leaving us to do whatever there was to do. I gather there are lots of humans on their home planet, as well. Relations appear to be guardedly amicable. "Economic partners", we are now, we're told. I don't know any, not personally. The atmosphere is breathable again; good, in fact. Better, cleaner than before.

For a time, I'd thought the future was meaningless, would be non-existent for me without Bouncy – Saritor and his sparking wit. And… and *everything*. But you have to live, and that takes time and effort and thinking and you don't have the energy to spare for anything else.

Staring at the screen, I feel ill now. I don't need memories like these… dreadful times in the cellars, looking after the fighters and fleers, feeding them… nursing and doctoring them. Bouncy was one of the patriot fighters. If I wasn't mopping the blood from his body, I seemed to be mopping it off the floors. So he called me Moppy, and I called him Bouncy: there he was, night after night, day after day. Him and his unquenching drive. His absolute luck in surviving so long. Even the Qinting called him Bouncy – they must have thought he kept bouncing back on them, too. Their word was Saritor – it sounded better in Qinting.

❄ ❄ ❄

Terrible times and days… awful happenings. But so much sheer excitement – the edges we lived on! The thrills. Every day. Every moment living at three hundred pc. By the Towers of Hyriad! To have those

159

days back… those nights. Saritor was the only one I ever loved, with that battered, muscled body. We bedded when we could. He was so strong. Such courage. Born leader. So much did I love him…

And here he is – the other end of an ii-link. It has to be him – the Real Saritor. No-one else knows I was Moppy.

It's burning inside me, even now, that feeling for him. So easy to let it rise. Bring back those life-bursting times.

Yes, we bedded. Of course we did. So glorious amid all that destruction and killing. Too hectic, frantic, exhausting and everything else for the passion to be exactly rampant. But such heights we seemed to reach! Nothing since had quite touched it yet. *Be honest, girl – nothing's come close.* Adrenalin under the rags, we called it. Not constant or unceasing, but it was often enough to be a glory every time.

Yes… often enough: Cailita and Coronella, his twin daughters, are playing behind me; seven years old, almost eight. My two cees.

He's on the other end of this link. I could… We could. Yes… yes. Soaring within…

I reach forward. I press the key. Slowly and deliberately, knowing exactly what I'm doing. There's no way I'm going to dig up the bones of the past; or allow the bones to come and dig at me.

I've cut the link. It fades fast. I turn to my two Cees; and my five Bees – Burni, Bryun, Benni and Barick; mine and Benjamin's little boys.

No way could I ever… I gaze at them. 'You know how you've been mithering to move away from this place? This district, with all its memories for me?'

They stared up at me, all so big-eyed and beautiful. 'I think I'm ready to leave here now. What say we emigrate to the sun, sea and sand of Hatana? Prasap1.'

PUPPETMASTER

Dad was really funny at my birthday party. Like after we'd had all the party food and some games and watched a cartoon on Netflix. And then he did his special show of the glove puppets talking and playing tricks. He said he bought them from a man on the market selling them out of a suitcase, but they were the only two he had left.

'All his other stuff was silken scarves, and strings of beads, and silver bracelets,' Dad said.

He had Ralph the Rabbit on his right hand, and Larry the Lamb on the other one.

They were super-funny with all their jokes and weird little voices and conjuring tricks that he could do. He was everso good, and really enjoying himself, by the looks of it. I didn't see his lips move once. Dad was magic with them.

They were stuck on his hands, he said, 'They're too tight. My wrist must have swelled.'

I saw him trying really hard to pull them off.

He was cursing them like he did with the man who messed up the plumbing last week.

I heard him in the night. I think he was walking about. He does that sometimes since my mum went away.

In the morning he didn't come into our room to wake us up to go to school.

So we stayed in bed till it was getting really late. Then we went in to wake him up, so he could come and wake us up in time for school.

He wasn't there.

But Ralph and Larry were on the bed, and they were absolutely *huge*.

SECOND THOUGHTS

In the dark. In bed, thinking about Madelya, beside me, so warm and silky soft and smooth. I lightly stroke. The darkness hides her smile. Or maybe she isn't smiling; perhaps she frowns, or regrets. And me? What do I think? Well, there's a first time for everything. Or first *few* times, I suppose. A couple – at least – last evening in the euphoria. Certainly, sometime in the depth of night, when the air had been so still and quiet; not a murmur from anywhere.

And again just now as we awoke. Or had she been awake already? I have no idea what her sleeping routine is. Not that this liaison is routine for her, either. Does she usually lie in? Or sleep briefly before starting work around the home?

My hand seems to roam where it will, unbid. Am I feeling a little shy or awkward now? Is she? Why? We were perfectly open last night, and in the afternoon and evening, as things developed and we both understood more… about each other, and all manner of mutual things and interests.

'Jeems, you do have such wondrous breasts. Would you… er?'

'Mmm, yes…' Her hand – such long, delicate fingers – came to me. Her higher breasts so superbly full and rounded. The middle pair so pert and firm… the lower ones not yet matured. Her infinitely fine fur had retracted as she slept, her skin now so ivorine.

As I touch, I gaze blindly in the blackness to where her cute snub nose must be, scarce a span away, and those eyes – the front ones so green as a rule; the rear ones, more inclined to see in UV light than visible, probably monitoring the room now. The lack of external ears isn't ever noticeable, not visibly. But, as I stroke through the cascading beauty of her long, zebraic-striped hair, it occurs to me that her skin-flush aural membranes must be there somewhere.

'Second thoughts?' she quietly asks.

'No.' Sure, I'm aware of the momentousness of the occasion – a first for both of us, and much more than one night together implies. No, *implies* is a wriggle-out word. It was stated and agreed: we are committed to giving it a go – no second thoughts. After working together for more than two deccadays – nearly thirty days now – Madelya and I know each other's thinking and abilities fairly well. Very much the same vein of humour, too: we laugh at the same things, and at the same people around the complex. We work well together; and have mentioned setting up as independent operators a couple of times.

I know it seems a mite precipitous, but each of us knows the ins and outs of the business: she's bright in mind and outward in attitude, and we've been planning and preparing to team up for a decca. Actually setting it up for four days. And bed? Well, since sometime post-noon yesterday, I suppose. We'd both known we would.

Yes, this whole thing is pretty momentous: inter-species partnerships aren't unknown in business matters. They're rare in personal lives, though. Maybe a first in this part of Shiruki: it's one of the more conservative planets in this sector.

A noise outside distracts me. I pause to listen.

'Ignore them. It's just the humans across the hallway. They do quite a lot of this, too.'

I uncoil my tail, and wrap it around her body – her back responding divinely as her light down eases out of her silken skin. So delicate on the down-stroke, so arousing against the nap. Oh yes, life's good. No second thoughts for me.

Now… Which penis should I use this time?

SELF-LEVELLING

Jaimie cursed – and he's not one for cussing as a rule. 'Hey! Has some sodding kid just walked across there?'

I went over to the area he was laying – we'd done the main concrete base together last week, flooded the whole ground-floor almost up to the damp-proof level. Not that they were rooms as such, not yet: we'd built the foundations and reached up to just over ground level. Our neat double lines of brickwork marked out what would soon be rooms as the courses rose each day.

Today we'd taken a room each. The plastic damp-proof membrane from Screwfix was easy to spread, and we started on pouring the self-levelling compound and spreading it round. A couple of centimetres deep was all, so it was easily achievable in a day. Sure, they call it self-leveller, but it needs spreading and smoothing, just the same.

There was the subject of Jaimie's anger – a set of small footprints cutting diagonally across his room-to-be. Coming in off the future back garden, and leaving via the left side. The bricks were only a centimetre higher than the self-level surface with its little trail of new footprints. Hardly a barrier to even a small child.

'You didn't see anybody?' I asked him. 'Little kid?'

'Nothing. I'd swear nobody came through here – the site's got the perimeter barriers up, anyway.'

'Well, whatever... I'll give you a hand to re-smooth it. You want to take the side bit, and I'll start at the far end?'

I went round to where the little footmarks started, and he went where they ended. 'You notice, Jaim? They're barefoot.'

He stood there a moment. 'Kids,' he said, and we both knelt to get started. 'Oh bugger. The footprints. Pete. Look.'

A new set of little foot marks was coming towards me. I felt so stupid. I know my mouth was sagging open. Heading straight for me. Determined little pace. I dropped sideways so they didn't walk into me, and felt more stupid. They reached the edge right next to where I was sprawled out and didn't slow at all. They'd run out of wet leveller to walk on.

I stood up, and we simply stared at each other. We looked round to see where the creator might have gone, then the other way to wonder where it might have been to for a few minutes.

Neither of us knew what to do or say. We looked at each other. 'I didn't really see footprints make themselves just now, did I?'

'If you didn't, I didn't.'

'We'd better get this done, then, before it sets.'

'Yeah,' I said. 'They'll leave dimples even if it self-levels. You want to grab the bull float? It'll reach the middle part from there.'

We started smoothing the marks away. I slipped my float trowel across the furthest marks I could reach, and Jaimie was managing the rest with the long-handled float. 'What do you reckon it was?' he said. 'Ghost?'

'No idea.' I knelt up, finished with my bit. 'Maybe like another dimension, they go on about?'

'I heard of them. So… What? You reckon we've just brought this floor up to the same level as theirs? This other dimension? Their world?'

'How would I know? What are we going to do about it, Jaim? Anything?

'And say what? They'd think we were nuts. Especially now we've cleaned away the evidence. That floor'll be solid set in an hour.'

I had a bothersome thought. 'D'you think they'd make us stop work while they investigate?'

I could tell Jaimie didn't like the idea of that, either. He weighed it up. 'Can't imagine anything's going to happen again. Not once this surface's dry.'

'Yeah, that's true. Not going to leave a mark when it's all gone solid, are they?'

'What we going to do, then?'

'How big a prat do you want to look?' He didn't seem keen on his mates thinking he was going nutty; he pulled a face.

'Okay,' I said, 'Let's get this levelled, then go for a pint in the In Between. And say nowt to *anybody.'*

THANK YOU, MELLISSA

'It doesn't make sense, Mrs Scapisky, when I think of how things happen around me.'

Mrs Scapisky was not happy with me, and became rather sarcastic. 'Well, we all know that things happen differently around *you,* Mellissa.' And she carried on telling us about different forces and objects and states of matter.

I said again, 'But I don't think that's right.'

'Do not interrupt or contradict me,' she said crossly. 'Thank you, Mellissa.'

So I listened to her telling it all again and still didn't see how she could possibly be right. I said so when we went for our afternoon wee and milk break. I thought she was going to hit me. Just for saying I saw things a little differently to how she did.

Sarcastically again, she called me Ine Stine.

I would not have understood sarcasm last year, but I'm five now, and when I told my dad what the canteen ladies had said at Christmas, he explained to me about sarcasm and how people with very small minds use it to belittle – I think he said belittle – people who know more than them and they don't want to admit it.

So on the way back to class, after I'd washed my hands and face, I said, 'It's not nice to be sarcastic to small children, Mrs Scapisky. I don't think you ought to do it in class.'

She grabbed hold of me by my shoulder.

I was very surprised. It made me yelp. She was quite red and angry then, and marched me into class. She let go of me right at the front where she always stands and said, 'Alright then, Little Miss Knowall, let's hear your version.'

I straightened my dress and said, 'You shouldn't grab hold of children like that, Mrs Scapisky. I would have come. You only had to ask.'

So, I faced the class, 'Well, children.' They were all looking at me and I didn't know if I could explain it to them. I mean, they were only eleven and twelve – the teachers keep making me leave my friends and go up a class, so they're all older than me.

'I would like to thank Mrs Sca— Er… Firstly, there is no such thing as different forces. There is only one force in the whole universe. We can call it energy – or Fred, I suppose it could be. It's everywhere. Except where it hasn't got to yet because it can't move fast enough to have gotten to places that don't exist yet. They only exist because energy has got there.'

'Yes, but—'

'Please don't interrupt or contradict, Mrs Scapisky. Energy is everything, and it can change its form. It can spread itself out really thin and we say it's gravity. Or really, *really* thick like in black stars. It can change from one sort to another, but it might not be easy. Like light and heat can change just like *that*—' Oh, shoot! I can't click my fingers however much I practice.

'And lumps of energy can change to light and heat like in atom bomb things. So they must be able to change back.

174

And all the states of matter – I think there must be a lot more than gas, liquid and solid – at least seven or eight or ten more. I think they can change whenever they want.' I had a sip of water before I carried on. 'And time as well. Time isn't just when we come to school or go home for tea. No – it can change and go fast or slow, depending on how fast we're moving. I bet it can change into other things as well. I think time's just another sort of energy like light and gravity.'

'But time's different…'

'No, it's not, Tony Millkins. You're not listening. It's all *energy* – it just shows itself in different ways – like solid hard lumps – which are nearly all space but with very concentrated energy holding the bits together. And time and gravity change up and down together so they must be…' I wasn't sure what they must be. 'I'll have to think more about that,' I told them. 'And they make matter change as well. Yes – like time and gravity, and space-ships getting all stretched out on the way into black holes.'

Ogbo Mgbu said something really silly about his scab had matter in it and I ignored him and sniffed like Mrs Scapisky does.

I admitted I didn't know exactly how electrics and magnets fitted in – but it was obvious they did, especially with light, and so it must be with gravity and time as well. 'I expect energy shows itself according to what mood it's in – it might be feeling timely or plasma-y, or a bit gravity-ish. Like Mrs Scapisky might be feeling sarcastic-ish… Or really lovely and magnetic…' I had to say that because I saw the expression on her face. I thought she was looking a bit lumpy, like lead, actually.

'Yes, but we all run out of energy, Mellissa.'

'We don't really run out of it, Mrs Scapisky, we turn to different sorts of energy like smoke and heat; or worms and maggots. All our energy gets spread out and other people can use it, or it can even shine into space, where aliens might use it. And when the sun changes itself and blows everywhere—'

'Thank you, Mellissa.'

'But I haven't finished, Mrs Scapisky. I haven't told you about—'

'It's time to start our writing now, Mellissa. And don't tell me that time is fluid and I could change it. Hmm?'

'No, Mrs Scapisky.' Shoot! I *was* just going to say that.

'I expect the universe will run out of energy before you do, Mellissa.'

'Oh no. The universe will never run out of energy. I think it must all be changing to one sort that's spread out perfectly evenly everywhere. I think they call it entropy.

'Actually, I wonder if that's the opposite to what was before the Big Bang? Because then, *all* the energy was in a point the size of *nothing*. Perhaps when all the energy is used up and spread everywhere, it like bounces back and starts going backwards towards being a nothing point again. Then it can all start again with another great Big Bang. And keep doing that for ever and ever.'

'Hmm. Thank you, Mellissa.'

Now that really is something to think about when I'm in the bath tonight.

I don't know where my yellow ducks came from, but it's funny how, when we talk to each other, they help me to get things straight in my mind. It's like they know *everything*.

THE KATERINI CATASTROPHE

It was a lovely sunny day. Little boy Helios Paplova watched the ants through his huge magnifying glass. They were so big. He could see their eyes and their little legs scurrying as he followed them. 'Wow.' He breathed in wonderment. 'They're enormous through the lens. If I move the glass backwards and forwards, they shrink or grow…'

Helios Solaris, watching the child, understood his thoughts and interest, his amusement. So, from far, far above, he decided to help. 'I'll sprinkle a touch more sunshine for the boy.' He could see the boy liked it. So he sent more…

Helios Paplova loved the warm, bright sun, and was happy for the ants. He watched them grow huge or small in his great lens. And at one specific distance, the sun's light came together in a white spot that made the grass suddenly wilt.

'Wow!' He jumped. One of the ants had shrivelled, and a tiny puff of smoke arose. Being an intelligent little lad, he realised what had happened. 'I'm going to try that again,' he ventured, and moved the lens to exactly the right distance to make a brilliant white spot on the ground. Sure enough, another ant vaporised. There was the slightest of aromas. 'It's like a lemon or something,' he said in surprise. As he was a mischievous little boy, an inquisitive one, he wondered how many he could do that to. 'Suppose I could make

179

them all go up in a puff of smoke and a nose-tickling smell?'

This could be exciting, 'Yes, that'll give them something to think about on such a nice warm day.' So he held the lens at just the right height, and played the white-hot spot through the mass that swarmed around the pinch of sugar he'd placed there.

∿

Helios Solaris saw this was a good game, and sent down more sunshine for his namesake on Earth. He liked the way the child pretended to be getting too hot in the extra sunlight he was sending – the way he sought the shade. So he sent down more and more sunshine from the great height of ninety-six million miles.

And more and more. Trees began to smoke… buildings caught alight… the lake boiled.

Oh, yes, he could appreciate how the boy had enjoyed doing this to the ants. 'Most rewarding,' he congratulated himself.

∿

The Katerini Catastrophe, as it became known, involved the deaths of over thirty-seven million people, burned to death over a period of one hour twenty-six minutes.

The *immediate* cause was determined to be the most intense beam of light ever recorded – estimated to be brighter than a helix-core laser by ten-fold. It slashed across the land, and the houses and people across the whole of the Central Mediterranean, centred on northern Greece. Rivers evaporated in great bursts of steam. Farms and villages, towns and cities vanished with no trace.

'The *root* cause is still a total mystery,' the scientific conference concluded a year later, in their final press release. 'We remain baffled by a phenomenon which had been undreamed of, and cannot be explained by any known set of factors in the realms of normal physics, quantum mechanics or quasar relativism.

THE LIVING WALL

'It's been empty for seven floogling years?' I said. '*Seven?*' I knew the Mikros were short in stature, but this hinted that they were lacking in the intelligence and decisiveness departments, too. 'And you wait till now to try to find out why? This was a crisis six years ago – not today. You've gone from an emergency to a last hope – and you resort to an agent like me. Well,' I gazed down at my companion, 'you appointed the right person to find out exactly what the reason is.'

'And the solution,' he reminded me, allowing himself a weak, plaintive smile.

There it was, towering across the end of the valley like an enormous dam – The Living Wall. An architectural masterpiece, or so the Mikro publicity had boasted for the past seven years. A curving, gently-sloped cliff face of a building twenty stories high, and twenty-eight apartments wide. Artistically shaped to echo the curve of the rolling hillsides that surrounded it; the panoramic windows a classic of functional design and aesthetic appeal. When new, it was a stark, pristine wall of brick, rock and glass, but quickly took on its Living aspect...

The Living bit? A sub-balcony at each level planted with ivy, creepers, villi and sunsuckles. 'In the past seven years, they spread, and clung to the walls over the residential balconies in drapes and reaching fingers,' The rep told me. 'In the summers, when the front face caught the full hot glare, the wall was a sea of colour-flashing flying life – kakadus and papugi, mostly. People liked the look of it, and we weren't allowed to trim it all back; maintenance cash dried up, anyway.' He shrugged – the way they do.

Still not understanding the reason for the building's emptiness, he pulled a face, 'It's one of the wonders of the city – in the top ten for tourists – beautifully merged swathes of pastel colours across its face, largely hidden by the creepers and birds after all these years untrimmed.'

'Yes,' I agreed. 'Towering there with such fine views, over the forest and rocky wilderness, down into the whole spread of the city.' The swathes of silvery buildings and copper-coloured spires of the city caught the sun's rays in early mornings and late evenings… the Science and Techno District with its equally ultra-modern buildings… the Aranganta-tree Park… the clustered pinnacles of the old town…

The Living Wall gazed over them all.

'We expected it to be a most desirable residence – See? In the distance, you can see the Stellar Tower alongside the Sub-orbital space-port. There are unrivalled views of incoming and lifting-off craft.'

'Indeed so. It truly is a wonder.'

'They come in droves, the tourists from Elquentor who land at the space-port centre, to vid the Living Wall, selfie it, upload to their off-planet sites and friends and families. Occasional ones simply marvel at it. But we have no idea why no-one wants to buy an apartment, rent one, or take a hotel room. And that's despite it being designed according to the most modern understanding of our off-planet tourists and friends. Not one single person has ever moved in. The designers expected they would be falling over each other at the chance of a second or third home, or short-stay hotel environment.'

'And you waited seven years to do something about it? All that money and time invested in it? It's a disgrace to you and the city. So are you.' No point smudging my words.

Their excuse had something to do with an off-planet investor, a series of owners and law cases, conflicting intentions… The Living Wall had practically become a write-off before it was started. Only recently freed from legal and financial restraints, they wanted advice on what to do next.

I was back ten days later. 'It's the Elquentorians who're your target tourists? Rich and up-coming? Yes? Well, they don't like to be high up – they're ground-level people at home. So living more than a floor into the sky is a total bù-bù. Got to be ground level. Yes, I know they have high-rise blocks on Elquen, but only for work, not for living in – they're deserted at night – won't sleep in them. The counter side is that they also refuse to have anything on top of them, such as twenty stories of concrete and glass, steel and brick. So being in the lower floors is equally a zilch proposition. They would either feel crushed or floating-dizzy.'

'But… but… Kirim'sip'sid, the designer had much experience with our target buyers – I mean, honoured guests from Elquentor. He lived and worked there many years, had many friends there, and consulted widely.'

'Hmm,' I said, with extreme dubiousness. 'I trust he died of viral incompetence?'

'Do you have a proposal to remedy the situation?'
'I do. All is not totally lost.'

They didn't like it, but I said I was prepared to put all my own savings into my proposed venture to rectify the problem. About a thousandth of what they'd need to invest, but I was pretty sure it would work.

'We build eleven hundred single-story homes behind the Living Wall.'

But they'll only see the rear of the Wall: there'll be no view over the city.'

'Of course not,' I agreed. 'Yet. You build all the homes, then knock the Wall down. Or, actually, blow it up. Get rid of it as spectacularly as possible. When you've started building, get your advertising people on to it. Announce a grand demolition – or Grand Demolition in capital letters, gold-plated and neon-lit. This will be the event of the decade, The Great Unveiling of The View from their own homes. The occasion will be restricted to purchasers; as will the view thereafter. You will stage a magnificent, and very-well publicised, demolition of the Living Wall – in Autumn, when the birds have flown south. Or we will. I'd put my own money into it if you're short.' I perhaps shouldn't have said it quite like that – they're all short, size-wise.

They went for it, and wrote off the fortune that had slowly wasted away over the past seven years. They built a whole colony that drifted in steps and swathes up the forest and rock hillside behind the Living Wall. Our low-rise estate was a silver cascade down the valley-side. Each bungalow had the same panoramic windows as the apartments in The Wall. In truth, many of them were the same windows – they had been removed to save on costs.

My genius stroke was to be the demolition of the Living Wall – it would give those clear views to the thousand-plus dwellings across the hillside – views of nature – the newly-planted Aramasque tree groves so they could gaze on natural beauty, and the Ponya Lake... the Park of Elquen... presently hidden, but to be exposed when the Living Wall came down.

The spires and towers of the city would peek above them – a tantalising glimpse of what was beyond – the far spread of the city and the space port. And The Demolition – the creation of their view – would be the fabulous birth of their community. The system-wide publicity, and demolition-raffle, the sale of souvenirs, rubble, living pics, holos and vids, front-row seats – or front-row views from the new single-story dwellings

Every last no-rise home sold pre-completion, and they were all occupied in time. Everyone wished to be there from the outset – such is the power of one-upmanship advertising. Occupants would be able to brag that they were here that day – from the very commencement, the grand unveiling, the moment the great Living Wall was removed like a curtain falling to reveal the beauty beyond. They needed to be there – once the advertising convinced them of it. To witness The Revealment.

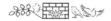

So, if this works out right – and it looks as if we'll make a handsome profit overall – we have two other

sites earmarked for a similar wall building, which can be constructed immediately prior to the constructions of the swathe of hillside dwellings behind it. So much cheaper and faster to build the next Living Wall without rooms or stairs or lifts or utilities, just an impenetrable but temporary block to their view. Designed to explode or collapse like the falling apart of a vast theatre curtain, with appropriate fanfares, fireworks and celebrity guests and artists. All vidded and broadcast through the Fed.

Okay, so we won't be able to do it too often – although the Elquentorians seem to know exactly what's going on, and pretty much approve of the whole concept of the "Birth of a Community" with a Grand Unveiling of The View.

We're currently undertaking initial surveying and market research on three other planets.

THE WELCOME MATT

'Boss?' Dakk sidled into my officio magnum. 'There's another refugee craft come into orbit – an hour ago.'

Oh, hello. The way he's apologising his way in, there's something up with this one.

'Humanoids, are they? Humanic class? Or Total Diffs? More Carapacids, are they? Do we know where from? They been in contact yet? Tried to claim anything?'

'Well… er… they're Grentals, from Verdil.'

That says it all - Grentals. 'Are they still at war over there?'

'Sure are – and the last craft we accepted, you'll recall, was the Extoradi, former servant slaves of theirs.'

'They needn't continue their wars here. If the Extoradi can put their differences aside, anyone can.'

'There's still bad blood between them, Boss. And not just the blood – the Grentals object to facial characteristics, too – Large ears… snub noses. If we let them download, we'd better keep them well clear of each other.'

'You know the policy, Dakk: if you can't mix, you can't land.' He was edging… he wanted me to take this one.

'I'm still processing the Wingies from Dew,' he was excusing himself. 'Hardly understand a word they chirp, but they're looking pretty well-suited. But with this Grental one, I'm getting an ominous feeling.

189

Would you mind taking it yourself, Matt? Please, Boss?'

***

I transferred their senior team onto Orbit Platform One for initial processing. Team? Ha! – their loudest rabble, more like. Four of them, I went and sat with. I could scarcely get a word in, for all their caterwauling and demanding. The list of things they insisted on, swore they needed, 'We cannot possibly tolerate the provision of anything less than this.'

Watching them, I let their demands wash over me. There had been a time when their greenish skin and lack of a neck would have raised my hackles, but not for years. On Atlast, we don't allow ourselves any prejudice – there was too much trouble here in the past; and in other places and spaces now. We can't afford bother. We're on the pov-line

They were opening their own airlock with their stipulations – who they'd be prepared to live with – definitely not near Totals of any kind – and there'd be trouble if they were housed with red-bloods or slit-eyes. They had a list of their minimum requirements – kind of food… own homes…

My usual sigh. I listened and recorded for the required one hour while they put their case for asylum, and agreed their commitments. 'Koh… My turn. We are a poor planetoid—'

'You think we don't know that? Think we came here by choice? Scrugging scabrag – get us somebody senior to give us our rights. Never mind all this shiko. We want moving on to Central.'

'Right,' I told them, 'let me summarise this for the recordings, hmm? You won't live near Totals, nor share districts with Elkons or Extoradi. Bearheads, too, hmm? Nor do any kind of work that involves hard physical exertion; or overly demanding mental activities. Your women do not work at all? And you need a minimum of four deccas to acclimatise, recover from the hazardous voyage here and settle in to your new communities?

'Koh, now—'

They interrupted – all of them at once. *Well-practised,* I thought.

'No! Be quiet!' I told them. 'It's my turn. Allow me to outline our position here on Atlast. We are a small outlying colony of Central. We have no Central support – which means we survive or not by our own wit and labour. Barely, so far, we survive. We welcome like-minded beings of *any* kind. And I mean exactly that. All beings who are like-minded are welcome.

We have six Total Diff communities – all integrating with no undue difficulties. We are home to two Carapacids – two different Wingies... an aquatic-preferring population we call the Peschids, though they call themselves Glugglety click-click, or something of that nature. However, they work and fish, communicate, trade and mix in as best they can, and are not a burden. There's also the Elasmo Torides – Lazzies – who have, entirely of their own volition, found a niche in the hunting and forestry areas, and seem to be thriving, with excellent economic and semi-social relationships all round.

'There are also eleven communities that are basically humanoid or humanic – apart from we original Blues, of course... Yes, as you say, we're the Bluey Long-necks. Do feel free to be insulting when you're applying for—

'No – you're not *claiming* anything. There are no rights here. I have no rights, other than what my work earns for me, even though I have thirty-eight years seniority. Two more to go and I gain full citizenship. We need to be of value to the community before it will value us.

'Everyone starts with nothing. All of us Originals included. No no… that's how it is. You work, and earn account markers… tokens, vouchers or credits which you can exchange for food, shelter, heating, recreation. You can save them up for other things you want.

'But it starts with work. No – your craft has very little value to us – we don't want to go anywhere. Besides, we have two dozen or so similar ones in static orbit already. It would simply park here with the others – no actual use to us.

'Prelim handouts? Start-up grants? Transitory period? Exemptions? Choice of accommodation and region? Special foods? No no no. I've already told you – you've got the wrong idea about Atlast – we're a struggling frontier post of what used to be the Central Empire. Nobody brings their homeland, racial and species wars here – No! You don't. They're of no significance here – the only important thing here is that you earn your keep.'

'We have rights—'

'Shut up about rights! They don't exist. The only right we grant you is that you can turn round and go away, before this interview is concluded and a decision is made. If you wish to remain here, I just told you the conditions. No, you can't see someone else. No-one

else will see you. And if another officer had happened to be dealing with you, they would have told you exactly the same thing. It's our law. We don't need Central to tell us. We're on Outer Province Law here.

'"You fit in or you fuck off." See? It's written on the wall emblem behind me. It's Atlast's immigration motto. FioFo.

'No no – we can *not* afford freeloaders. There is no time period for adjustment. If you want to eat – you work. We don't have stocks of spare food. You grow it, catch it, raise it, trap it or exchange for it. That's it. Someone had to build the shelters – you need to work to pay them back for their efforts.

***

I left them to it. They'd been travelling twenty-some days from Verdil... been at war with the Downies – or whatever they called each other – just because they have a fine down instead of body hair. But some folk get turned over by *their* green shade – or our blue tint and long necks. The No-Ears, for example...

All we humanics can interbreed: it's what defines us as humanic. Some people here have even set up house and work with *non*-humanics – Total Diffs – especially the Elasmos. I've even heard about some of us Blues setting up together with Wingies. No, I don't want to know what they get up to, if anything. I think they just *understand* each other; they gel with each other's attitudes or something. Seems to work for them.

But the Greenies – the Grentals – seem to think everybody and everything that's not just the right shade of jade is an inferior – born to be their slave.

***

They've had their two days to decide. I've spoken with more of them, lots more. Almost everyone paraded the same attitude: 'We have come here to escape persecution...'

We're not having non-Grentals ordering us around...'

'The whole concept of being required to perform physical labour is abhorrent to us...'

'Our women cannot be expected to work...'

They openly sneered at me, 'You're a mere underling. We don't mix with Blueys... especially you long-necks.'

Three of them, all women, came to me separately, and said they would willingly accept our rules, with their children, rather than be asked to leave, if they weren't going to be forwarded to Central.

'You're not. No-one ever goes to Central. It's too far for the provisions and power reserves your ship has. And even Central has been badly affected by the Wars. It's not policy to tell everyone, but it seems that Central is in a worse state than we are – I heard they shoot incomers on first sight, rather than risk a drain on their resources, infection or foment.

'But, if you truly mean that you want to stay here, you would need to work exactly as I said. You would pay for your children's food and care – although there are allowances for children. Could you do that? Any others among you?'

The women talked about it among themselves.

***

Their decision time is up. I'm having the Grental craft shunted into static parking orbit, slotting neatly among a procession of previous newcomers.

194

What happens next is entirely of their own making. I have followed our legal procedures to the key-press – as agreed in our inter-planetary treaties, including full discussion with a colleague to confirm our interpretations. Dakk was fully prepared to back me up on every count; he'd seen what was coming, and hadn't wanted to take on the primary responsibility himself.

'I'm a negotiator,' he said. 'And there's not much negotiating to be done. They are not welcome here.'

'They failed the statutory tests, so we categorically cannot permit the whole manifest of crew and passengers to settle here on Atlast.'

'And that also means they will not be permitted to leave.'

'It's why we formed the Outer Colonies Mutual Support Network when the Wars broke out.' I signed the plasdocs and passed them to him. 'If one of us rejects a ship, we all do. And we take care of it, rather than having an aggressive demandee trying to get to somewhere else that also can't afford to pamper intolerant factions.'

Dakk sighed, and signed. 'Fourteen women, eighteen children, and one man decided they did want to settle here on our terms. I can keep them together, at least for a period. Then it's up to them. They'll start the induction for their new jobs at the sixth hour in the morning, tomorrow.'

'And at precisely the same time, alongside the twenty-nine ships that are already neatly parked in static orbit, the Verdil Star will suffer a sudden and catastrophic air loss, and become the sixth coffin up there.'

'Will you tell our new citizens?'

195

'Not yet. I reckon they're intelligent enough to have a pretty good idea, anyway.

TO SOMERCOTES AND BEYOND

Well, yes, you're not the first to ask me that. People do sometimes wonder how a Lady of the Night, as the polite ones call me, ever managed to reach such an exalted position. Not that I met too many polite ones in my previous occupation anywhere between Milton Keynes and Derbyshire; and the depths of Ilkeston were only in my later times. 'These days, I have to survive on clients who aren't as fussy as they are in Northampton,' I told two of my new street-friends in Somercotes. 'And nor am I.'

I mean, for me to be chosen out of all the millions of other people!

They told me, 'You're the most qualified person we've ever met.' And that was from all the oodles and oodles of planets they'd visited. They didn't always say "visited" – Their word had conno-tayshuns – I think they say – of conquered, or colonised, or wiped out, depending on the in-Tone-ayshun they put on it. I used to know a really nice man in Derby called Tone. He was eversuch a big boy. Good customer.

I don't know how they chose me in the first place, not exactly. Or how they found me in the car park that first night. I asked them, 'Have you got some sort of "Find-the-right-one" sensor up there among all your other appendages and squiggly bits?' Some of his eye

197

stalks twizzled round his head as if they were trying to see what I meant.

Well, anyway, originally, I was doing a bit of filling-in for my friend Deidre in Somercotes one Friday night when I happened to meet the first one. Well, to me, it just happened, although I suppose they might have planned it. I expect they were doing a kind of recky, and just happened upon me. Although perhaps they sensed me, like I said. Whatever.

Oh, right, yes. Sorry. To get back to the subject— Ha, I'm usually groping round somewhere warm and dark when I say things like that. You were asking how come I'm the Lady High Ambassador for Earth in the All-Alien Council, weren't you?

'Yes, right. Well, I asked them that as well, when I got over the shock.

And when got over the shock, they said, 'We've never met a human – or anything else – quite like you before.' And their antenners went a bit purply.

'You have yoo-neek qualiffy-cayshuns,' they told me. 'You're the most friendly and welcoming alien we've ever met.'

I had to tell them, of course, set them straight. '*You're* the aliens, not us.' Although, as I said at the time, we were in Somercotes, and it's easy to make a mistake like that. They all agreed that I reminded them of home with my baddy-narge-something. They meant my chat-up line and my total appreecy-ayshun of three-foot green todgers with bits on.

'We can tell you're not just being kind to us.'

Yes. No. Right. They have this thing about huge bosoms, too. Like mine. 'Well, of course they're inflated. Isn't everything these days, from balloons to the price of spermy cream?'

'Not just inflated,' one said. 'We can see inside you with the X-ray sensors on the tips of our sensicles.' They even quoted the implant patent number to me, and thought it was hilarious – the word Pat actually embedded inside both my boobs. Complete with a number that, apparently is the code for their launching procedure.

'Purely co-incy-dental,' I told them, though I always thought that had something to do with teeth.

'I think not,' they fondled back. 'It's clearly an omen. Always ready for Take Off,' they said.

'Not when I'm having my fish and chips, I'm not,' I told them. 'Unless you want to put the vinegar on yourselves.'

'We were only joking,' one squeaked, when I had him by the nuts and bolts.

But, anyway, it wasn't only that – me being part artificial – that swung it. Not those in-boob bits, anyway. That was just the start – When they found I had false teeth, they were ecstatic.

'That means you're actually, genuinely, part-alien,' they told me. 'Part android. That's wonderful.'

It's not like I'm shy about my fake bits – well, they're not fake. They're real. I paid for them. It's why I didn't create a fuss in the middle of all that Covid stuff we had, when I got run over by this tatty old Ford of all things. Wan't me doing anything – just walking my patch, but I ended up in Leicester Royal with my legs. I went in there with them, anyway. So I was lying round on this trolley while they dealt with all these folk with sniffles and coughs and stuff –

They got their priorities right in Leicester, haven't they? And when they got round to me, they said, 'You smell a bit.'

'Well you would if you hadn't been near a toilet all day,' I told them.

'No, it's not that,' they sniffed more. 'Something's septic.'

Yeah, right. My legs. Great. So I was whipped up to the operating theatre while they cleaned the surgeon up and wiped him down. And I said, 'Do a nice clean job, eh, Doc, I do a lot of walking.' I must have passed out then.

And you know, like, you wake up and you have no feeling that time's passed? But you know something's happened. Not like when some punter is really taking his time, and *nothing's* happened.

The "What's happened" in this case was my legs had done a runner. All on their own! Or *both* on their own, to be accurate.

I didn't mind very much – not at all, really. 'My new ones are really easy to clean on the bus after a rough night. And a girl needs a gimmick, doesn't she?' like I told the other girls outside the Sheep Herders' Arms. So that was when I moved up to Derby – they got loads of weirdos there and it's a kind of mutual attraction we have.

Which is why the aliens really took to me – cos I was attracted to their weirdo-ness. 'We have all kind of Weirdos and Beyond-the-Fringers on the All-Alien Council,' they said. 'And we just love all your pseudo-bits. It's as if you've been made, built and tailored especially for our tastes.'

'Perfect,' one said, 'just like my sister.'

'You don't?' I said, 'with your sister? But then, I remembered where I was and let it slide.

Before I accepted the post as Ambassador for Earth on the All-Alien Council, I had to ask them, 'Is it just a co-incy-thingy, or a hint about where all you aliens come from?'

'What's that?' Oggling-Ogberr said.

'The way "Alien" starts with the same letters as "Alfreton"?'

WHAT IT TAKES

'Unauthorised being at rear entrance. Do not admit. Repeat: Do not admit'

Why that stupid alarm has to repeat everything, and then tell me that it is a repeat, I have no idea.

'Shut up, Useless. Repeat: Shut up.'

'I am U.A.S.' she said, pronouncing it "You ass". She's a pain on occasion, and the rest of the time we're at war. 'I am not permitted to remain silent in the event of impending danger.'

'Silence Useless! You're as bad as my wife was.'

'I am not permitted—' A clout with an axle rod shut her up. What with a total lack of appreciation for all the extra pre-winter work, Useless whining indoors, and the wind moaning outside, my mood was not upbeat.

Purely to spite Useless, I jerked the rear door open, instantly lashed by freezing sleet, an early harbinger of my third ice-bound winter alone on Gaeaf since Marnie fled with the kids. No sign of— 'Ahh. There you are.' A beetle-furred koshka, half my height, 'You're the thieving, scavenging, vicious, diseased little snurk that's got Useless bleating, are you?' It was sinking to its knees, huge eyes looking up at me through the whipping sleet; wizened little face like a pinched nut.

'K'off.' I told it, thinking to aim a kick.

'Unauthorised being.' Useless shrieked her warning, as though this was some monster that was about to wreak ruination on my home – *Home? This?* A back-vac trading post, scrotel and bar? *This's home?* Complete with a UAS ordering me not to admit this pathetic, bedraggled little heap?

'Admission forbidden.' I wouldn't put up with a hysterical, argumentative ElectroGuard in my house, but United Assurance insist, because of all the stock in the retail areas and the bars.

Defiance ruled me, I beckoned. 'You coming in or not?'

'Do not admit.' It was worth it to hear Useless' hysterical doom-laden tone. 'This being is prohibited from entering the premises.'

Dripping wet, shuddering, shoulders slumped to nothing, it was silent as I tugged at its frozen-stiff canvas smock, exposing a double row of nipples among the frozen mass of straggly, knotted fur. 'You're female, huh?' I rubbed her down, careful of her dainty bits. Not a murmur or twitch, just big-eyed, fixated on my face. It could have been embarrassing, but it was an alien, more in common with beetles than humans.

'Useless. What do they eat?'

'Unauthorised being inside —' I was on my feet, Axle Rod raised. UAS capitulated, 'Fasolki beans.'

When I fetched it out the clothes-toaster, it – *she* – was looking fluffier, with light-tan fur. She sat, silently looking all around, before slowly spooning the refried beans down.

'Here.' I'd put a spare mattress on the floor, with covers, soupy drink and kids' clothes. *My girls won't be needing them, will they?*

'Useless.' I said. 'One squeal about this koshka, and I will remove your soul drive – got that?' I left them there.

It was one of *those* nights, me the jovial bar-keep; overnight roomies needed checking in, cash missing; kitchen problems… staff absent; over-exuberant truckers celebrating the Wheelers' 8-2 victory over the Toppers… Busy busy busy in this dreary dump with only a UAS for company. *Home? Huh.*

No thought or time for food in the early hours. Three hours so-called sleep, and I woke up remembering the koshka.

Dressed in kids' clothes, she was all big eyes and silent stare, looking as cute as my kids ever did. 'You can't stay. Out you go.' Silently, she looked into the dawn bleakness, the sleet hardened to ice. Her lower lip trembling, she tried to move, but couldn't. *Oh, Golgo. I can't physically kick you out.* I shut the door.

'Here…' Packet of refried fasolki beans, ten-second warm-up, clean dish and spoon, and I was away, checking day-staff turnout, the hardware sections, deliveries, a power downage, two non-starter rigs in the yard…

Grabbed a minute mid-afto – *she* was curled up in her corner. Had to smile. Like a tired-out kid. One eye opened slowly; thin little lips pursed; the eye closed. *You remind me of a pinched pine-nut.*

The pre-winter rush was building up – de-icer deliveries, a convoy of in-cab-sleepers, bar full of would-be drunks, power units to recharge... No time to eat.

So I slapped something on the cooksy towards midnight. Just for me, *No food, and she'll leave.* I looked outside. *Golgo's frozen nuts! Temp's ten down on yesterday. Maybe not tonight, huh?*

Sure enough, she wanted to leave at dawn. 'Okay. Off you go. Y' had a good deal.'

Useless wisely stayed silent about her while we went through the decc's accounts. I was kinda missing the little thing, though, until, 'Unauthorised being at rear entrance. Do not admit.'

Oh, Golgo's teeth. *She* was standing there, saucer-eyed, mouth opening in a silent sub-voc. I'm not that hard, so I nodded, and she was straight to her corner. All fur and baggy clothes, she watched while I did the meals. Half an hour later, lip-licking, pointy nose twitching, she curled up under the fake kemano furs.

Next morning, she wanted out again, but I watched as she scooted off round the oil sheds and was heading back like a rocket on afterburn within the minute. *Toilet spot back there, huh?*

She stood just inside staring up at me; that silent 'Ohhh,' again. Golgit – I stroked her head! Like she was a pet, not vermin.

Next morning, she was twitching on the mattress, whimpering and shuddering. I buzzed Kil Irton, who does the medicking at the mine-works. 'The Shivers.' He said when he saw her. 'The miners get it; dust mites in their ears.'

'She's got no ears.' Her smooth downy head trembled on the stuffed cushion.

'Course she has. Here, see?' He lifted a flap on the side of her head. A mass of writhing black lice beneath. 'Full-grown dusties – ready to lay. You need to chuck her out quick and fumigate the place.'

'No.' I out-stared him.

'Okay… We need to get all this scraped out her ears. They'll be deep in and clinging. She won't like it – the mining guys sure don't.'

So I held her over the utility sink while he did the scraping, and flooding with some vile-smelling tincture. She struggled at first – probably thought we intended to drown her, then bandaged her head till she looked like a religious lollipop on traffic duty. So wretched it was almost entertaining, she crept off to her corner.

'Everything'll need fumigating twice a day for a decca.'

'What?!'

I don't know how, but some of the ranch guys heard about me letting her in. 'Don't want no filthy koshies in here…'

'You get it out, or *we're* not coming in again.'

'Bye,' I said, and banned'em. 'This's my Post; my home. Nobody else got a say in anything.'

Before the decc was out, they were back begging, 'Lift y' ban, Frixy. Please. It's absolute *winter* out here; we need a drink.'

I stuck a note up saying first ban was one decc; subsequent bans would be four deccs; and then a year.' No bother since.

Doc Irton researched koshies' other illnesses, and inoculated and irradiated her against a host of possibles. She seemed grateful, undemanding and unprotesting, as though determined to be no more trouble. Keeping out the way, curling up on her own, peering into the ever-deepening snow and up at me before she scurried out twice a day. Ate the refries, drank the water, and sniffed at some of the meals I cobbled together.

One evening in the main bar, this brute of a logger woman comes sidling over. *You needn't bother*, I thought, *No freebies mid-decc.*

'I hear you got a koshka, Frixy? Couple of the loggies and drivers got'em, too. Bit of company on long drives, winter freeze-ins.

'You're telling me because?'

'Just wondering, Frixy, the side-bar don't get used much in winter... We thought we might... maybe... meet up? With our koshies? Hmm?'

Other people keep verminous aliens? It took five seconds to decide, 'Yes. Topday? Noon onwards? Half-price beer. Free fasolkis.'

She sat back. 'Y' not serious? Just like that?'

'Topday noon.'

I golging cried – *Sixteen* attendees, not just there for the ale and refries – loggers, miners, ranchers... drivers. Each with a koshka partner dressed in well-fitting clothing. It was like a coming-out party. We drank and talked, and our koshies mixed. Several brought vids, games, and stuff they could read – some could speak a few words! And liked to be stroked.

'Oh… Jipps – she's a little beauty, Frixy.'

'She is?'

'Absolutely. What a waif, though – underweight. Must be a year-old sprog. What you feeding her? Using a biddy, is she? Got some starter books? Zee-box games?'

'What's her name? She's a lost little creature without one, all alone in the world. Needs a name to belong.'

Evenings, nowadays, with music on, she often comes on my easicouch and curls up with me, ninety percent asleep, making this low humming sound, fingers flexing. She'll sometimes twist her head up and stare at me with those huge eyes, lips pursed for long silent moments.

'Worth your weight in relaxation, eh, my Yay-hesh, my Little Miss Softness?' I murmur. 'You've sure made this place something different...'

Tonight, her lips opened and she spoke her first word. 'Home,' she said.

ZYDD

Standing round in the bar of the Quaggan Dale, some Ku music playing, me and half a dozen of the fellers from work were having a call-in drink. We like the place for the décor, and the pics and vids of all the early planetary colonisation days – the original ships coming in, the domes, some really alien landscapes. There's a nostalgic feel to the place. Relaxing, having a laugh, arguing over the team selection for the cup match against the Squirrids. Sipping taiga tay – we pretend it's smart to drink that stuff, but it's expensive, so we only have the one before we move down the bars on New Vector Avenue for the rest of the night on something a bit stronger.

Yay! I'm lurching forward. Somebody shoved me in the back. Real hard. Deliberate. My fresh cup of t-t all down me and over the carpet.

'Don't you froiking dare say that about me.' Ranting behind me.

I'm still getting my balance, batting down my jacket at all the spillage, wondering what the shuffling shefters that was about. Some nutter? My workmates all open-mouthed and guarding their drinks – it's pricey stuff in the Dale. What? Who? I'm turning round, see who's accusing me of saying things about him.

It was one of the other guys – same sort of trade as us, on the hospitality side. Zydd, he was called. A Chitin – shell-back. He'd always seemed okay, pass the time of day with anybody. We've had a drink or two together in the past. But now, he'd really lost it. Raving at me. Deriding me for whatever – I'm an overgrown lump of something unprintable, apparently. Blaming me for some slight he thought I'd said. About him.

'I heard you. I know it was you.' Forehead stretching up and up – and furrowing down into his nose. That's when they're furious about something. Mouth in a snarl – row of teeth thrusting forward – really threatening, going at it. Practically frothing, he was. In fact, he *was* frothing. Huge eyes going dead black didn't help matters. I've never seen a Chitin anything like that wild before.

All my denials were in vain. It was humiliating. The others backed me up, 'He never said anything about you, Zydd.'

'Never mentioned you.'

'Talking about the match…' Trying to jolly him out of it.

But he was adamant: he wanted me out or there'd be real trouble – saying things like that about him. 'Always knew you were a shit.'

Me? He what? Where did that come from? We'd got on fine before. 'Come on Zydd, I never said a word about you.' But he was carrying on, getting a load of head-turners around him, all looking like they're blaming me. 'Okay, okay…' He's making a huge fuss, his claws flexing a bit too menacingly for my liking. 'I'm leaving.' Yeah, he was right out of it, gone all black-eyed and glittery at me, little compound facets flashing. Yep, he was beyond reason. He'd imagined something alright.

A minin later and we were all outside, heading down The Avenue a bit earlier than expected. The guys were saying, 'Forget it. We'll see him in a day or two.' But I was burning with it. So embarrassing. Somebody else might think I really had said something. Ruined my evening completely, and still fretting about it the day after.

**

I tried to talk with him when my next trip took me down the AstroDock, a week later. The MS Daisy Driller was off-loading there and I saw him, working on the bay. He didn't want to know. Lips pulling back, mouth-parts coming at me, all teeth. Claws extending ominously. It was like instant rage at me. So I backed out, apologising to my two mates, and we went down the Spacers' Arms for lunch instead.

**

It was the same on several more occasions over the months… One time, we were both on a job with a party of visitors to the twin sunsets on Tharyb…

Another time, we were doing some work in the same building…

One morning he was delivering to me…

The first couple of times I tried to say, 'Hi,' and follow it up with a comment about the weather, or the job, or the new gaffer on the City team. But he wasn't having any of it. He cut me off dead every time.

So I ignored him after that, and there was never a word between us. He lorded it round, bossy little shit with his team. I saw him mutter about me to some of the loader set. One told he was *really* bearing a grudge.

You ever see that viddy, *Antagonist?* Where one of'em blames the other for accidentally witnessing something compromising about her and she hounds

213

him over the years? It was like that with me and Zydd, but without the blood, guns and bare-arsed women.

After maybe a year of ignoring each other, or practically being spat at when we happened to meet face to… er… face, I simply avoided the localities I knew he haunted. But he always seemed to be there at the other places, too. It was always a downer. Every few months in one situation or another, we crossed glares. I suppose it was the circles we moved in – my transport, shipping and delivery job meshed with his catering and accommodation role, and we travelled round the same places.

A few times, I even thought about transferring off-planet, like when he'd been especially vocal about me at the yard one time… and in another bar in the dome. They even told us to take it in the vac if we wanted to be like that. 'I haven't even spoken,' I protested.' And I thought Mandible Malc who runs the Lobster Pot was a mate! 'It's the last time I smuggle a pack of fresh-froze prawks for you,' I told him..

But Zydd had high friends, influence around the port and I reckon I lost a couple of contracts through him interfering. There was no talking to him about it: the one more time I tried, he glossed, and greened-up really vivid, like he had done that first night.

It dragged on, became part of my background behaviour, like I'd spot him in the distance and cross the walkway, or not go in a place, or just wait till he'd gone. It was automatic, like ducking under a low beam in the cellars, or a permanent sniffle.

**

Then, one time, it was ages after the initial incident, maybe five years or so, I saw him down the All-

214

Species-Vet in Kaluushi. It was definitely him, looking unlike himself – gone was the blue-green lustre and erect shell-back spines. He was a pasty pink, all washed-out. Mouth sagging open, lips hanging. I never saw a Chitin looking that way before, either. Couldn't see what he had with him, half-hidden behind a cage. Something vile and dying, no doubt. *Good.*

I hated him. Glad he was down. Watched him for a time while we all waited for the Vetera to call the next one in. After ten mins, I was called, and went up the counter to pay for the inoculations for my Digby Parrots. 'Do you know Zydd? Saw you looking at him.' Danya was gazing up at me, all freckles, stripes and bulging boobs.

'I know him.' I put my dead face on. Didn't want any conversation involving him.

'Can you help him?' She says. 'He has to have his ocella put down. She's the same as your Kireina was – gorgeous old cat, big, old and striped. Might even have been out the same litter, from the looks.'

My Kireina? That's it, bring her up. Worst day of my life, having to have her put down after 21 years as my companion. She'd been stunning… beautiful looking, and her fur so soft. Gorgeous colour and patterning, whiskers like antennae. The sweetest-natured ocella there'd ever been – but everybody says that about their own, don't they?

'He's on his own,' Danya was going on, like I cared about him. 'His partner's not with him now – left or died, dunno. Got nobody to go in with him while they do it. Do you think you could?'

'No. I don't think so. We don't get on.'

I turned to go, but he was sitting there, one arm round his ocella. Froik! So much like Kireina had been. Lying, half curled-up, breathing really shallowly. Eyes not registering much. He was staring at the splash of drying haemo on the floor, dribbled from her. He sure looked hard-hit. I was like that when my Kireina— Froik, I went over and sat by him. He didn't look up. Sobbed. Even Mandy-head Kites do that, huh? Wouldn't have thought it. Silence, his claws slowly, rhythmically raking through the cat's fur.

Silence that stretched. Someone else was called in. The cat dripped another spot of saliva.

'Sorry about your cat, Zydd. Your ocella.'

He did look up. '*You.* You going to laugh? Or tell me you know how I feel?'

'Laugh? There's nothing funny about losing a twenty-year friend, and I don't know how you feel. I know how I felt. Still do. Never really got over it, I suppose.'

'Like you'd know.'

Okay, if you're going to be like that... But I stayed. If only because Danya had asked me to, and I wouldn't want her to think bad of me. Not with her freckles, stripes and things.

Talked a bit. Him sobbing about how intelligent... Only friend since... Did everything together. Never get another like her.

I didn't say a lot. He didn't want to hear someone else's grief or joys. Perhaps to share his own, I reckon. So I let him go on, encouraged him, I suppose, with an occasional prompt, of, 'Oh yes?' 'And then what?' 'Like she understood everything, eh?'

They called him through. He was trembling as he stood, picking her up, clasping her in his arms, his casings a-quiver, spines lying flat..

'I can come in with you,' I offered, 'if you like?'

He started away, stopped, and nodded, forehead furrowed low and stretched high. So I followed close and stood by his side while he cradled the striped creature. They conferred, him and the vetera. There was no alternative and we all knew it. I put an arm round him as they agreed the time was now. He pressed her close – just as I had done – and they pressed the lethal pad to her chest...

Barely a moment, her tail tip moved, claws flexed once, and she sagged slightly. And was gone. Her eyes lost their gleam. Stared for a few seconds before slowly closing for the final time.

They gave him plenty of time. Knew how it was for people. It was just as terrible a moment as it had been for me. But eventually, I caught a look from the vetera assistant who'd been hovering, and I said we ought to be going and he nodded again and let me lead him out.

His porter was outside but he wasn't in any state to drive it. I thought about it, for perhaps three seconds, 'Lemme drive you,'

'No. I'll walk.'

'Okay,' I wasn't up to arguing with him, so I made sure he did start walking. I didn't think he'd be safe if he changed his mind and came back for it. So I saw him out of sight down the ramps, then took myself back inside to collect my Digbys.

A couple of decs later, I saw him in the waiting area at the freight depot, cloistered with a few of his crowd. He looked half-recovered, lips covering his teeth, back spines up more, colour part-back. Not exactly sparkling and joining in. We met eyes and he looked down. So I went over at the midday break, 'You okay?'

He nodded. Didn't say anything. Didn't expect him to. No way we were going to be best mates. And I didn't want to be. Once bitten…

At least we're not cold enemies, either. I think maybe I understand a bit of what he went through.

218

He's not the type to ever say sorry for the years of being a bastard to me, nor thank me for being with him that day. Wouldn't expect it; wouldn't want it. It'd be embarrassing.

But I suppose he did, in a way: he turned up at a group I run for members of the Digby Parrot Partners Society. I heard him say to my helper on the door that I'd invited him, and had told him what great companions Digbys could be. 'Might I come in and see? And perhaps if I might be allowed to join your gathering? Find out… meet some members?'

'Of course.' Yessi, my helper was all welcome. 'We even have a pair of Digbys who have come along tonight, looking for a permanent companion and home.'

He was the only kite there, but a couple of the skinnies chatted with him and made him feel okay and introduced him round, including to the new Digby members…

I left them to it. One of the members was due to give a little talk and holo-experience about a Digby colony on Parravia. I watched and listened, opened up the bar for the after-talk social period, and seated myself to go over the membership list.

I was still buried in the subs and contact details when I saw a cup slowly descending to the table in front of me. It was carefully placed. A clawed hand turned it round. Adjusted it. Taiga Tay, I recognised the colour and aroma.

A voice mumbled, 'I owe you.'

THE AUTHOR

Trevor is a Nottinghamshire writer with many publications to his name, including reader-friendly books and articles about volcanoes around the world, and dinosaur footprints on Yorkshire's Jurassic coast.

His short stories and poems have frequently won prizes, and he has appeared on the television, discussing local matters.

In the 1980s, his research doctorate pioneered the use of computers in the education of children with profound learning difficulties.

Fourteen years at the chalkface; sixteen as headteacher of a special school; and sixteen as an Ofsted school inspector to round it off, his teacher wife regards their marriage as "Sleeping with the Enemy".

BY THE SAME AUTHOR

OF OTHER TIMES AND SPACES

Get a preview of the New-Classic Series with this giant-sized anthology. Thirty-nine highly entertaining and thought-provoking Sci-Fi short stories selected from the books of the New-Classic series. Over a thousand eBook pages filled with snappy two-pagers such as "Air Sacs and Frilly Bits" and "On the Seventh's Day" to the novella-length "The Colonist".

Could you keep ahead of "Melissa?", or manage an encounter "Of the 4th Kind"? From the laughs of "I'm a Squumaid" to the tears of "The Twelve Days of Crystal-Ammas", these are the best and most varied stories in the universe – according to eleven alien species and the author's mum. With two Sci Fi poems, two adapted stories from the trilogy novels "Realms of Kyre" and "A Wisp of Stars" and twenty-five illustrations.

Published in eBook and Paperback in Feb/March 2020

THE NEW-CLASSIC SCI-FI SERIES OF SHORT STORIES FROM THE LIGHTER SIDE

BOOK ONE - ZERO 9-4

At the 2039 annual all-species barbecue, it is confidently predicted that these tales will be unanimously voted the funniest and most thought-provoking sci-fi short stories in The Spiral Arm – the famous pub and restaurant on Ganymede – shortly before the Covid38 virus sends us all scuttling and slithering back to our socially-isolated orbits.

Could this be the future of homo sapiens in Cleanup, or Rigged and Ready, or in the poem Together Again? Are the aliens already among us in Betty, Kalai Alaa and Friday Night in Somercotes? What really happened the time his wife said Go for a walk, Oscar, dear?

Dare you immerse yourself in the laughs and trials to come in It isn't easy being a Hero, or Holes aren't my

Thing? Are you prepared to join the war of the alien genders in Kjid, or Typical Man?

If the Foundling in "Kyre?" can endure a skyfall into the forest swamp, encounters with a grallator, a pack of hounds, murderous soldiery and a supersensory woman, what destiny might await him, if he can run the gauntlet through the horde of rebel troopers?

Is They call the Wind Pariah a premonition of our fate in the grip of the Corona virus? Or is it in the hands of the scientists who believe the formula for space-time manipulation is Zero 9-4?

Fourteen illustrations light up the whole continuum.

More than half the stories are illustrated

Unleashed in eBook and Paperback in July 2020

BOOK TWO - ORBITAL SPAM

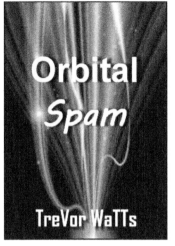

You've been dumped in the orbital spam folder, so what do you do about it, before the whole orbit is deleted? Is there anything you can do when the Great Pondkeeper up in the sky decides to call time? What is it that's Come Again on the agricultural planet of Kalèdas, just when the seasonal workers and left-over troops are readying themselves to leave?

If you receive the Prasap1 call, totally out the vac, are you going to answer it? While concreting the base within the single-brick-high walls of the new pub, what are you going to do when a trail of disembodied footprints determinedly heads straight for you across the wet surface in Self-Levelling?

From the laughs of Puppetmaster, I Can Only Take So Much, and To Somercotes and Beyond, to the poignant stories of What it Takes, First Call, Last Call, and Zydd these 20+ brilliant tales will alter your view of the future that awaits, whether Out There, or here on Earth.

Includes:

− an episode in the life of Kyre, Into the Arena, adapted from the fantasy trilogy, Realms of Kyre;

225

- three tales – The Katerini Catastrophe, Thank you, Mellissa, and Second Thoughts – that are included in the giant preview anthology, Of Other Times and Spaces;
- one poem: the beautiful, mysterious and stranded Mirador;
- illustrations to brighten any boring wait at the space-port, or leisurely evening in orbit.

Launched September 2020 in eBook and paperback.

BOOK THREE - TERMINAL SPACE

When it comes to that vital First Contact moment, do you think you'd have a better strategy than the occupants of the SS Stella Nova, in Polly? What on Earth can the alien do when he's stuck in traffic and going to miss his spaceship home? Find out why they call the Khuk spaceport's entrance tunnel The Terminal Space, when Prisoner 296 is sent in there to carry out repairs at rush hour.

Twenty+ stories of here and now, wondering what's among us; and the not-too distant futures and regions of space; or in the far-strewn arms of the galaxy where humans exist no more. Laugh with some, smile at others, or catch your breath at the trials that some have to face. Whether you shed a tear, or cheer them on, you can't help but find yourself immersed with these souls of universes to come.

How might you react if your people have been "Ruffled up a little"? Would you be up to answering Ĝemanta's heartfelt plea from Orbit Sphere 4X to Maar'juh'rih, the agony aunt? Do you believe you'd still feel like joining the war against the Nemican forces if you were informed that you were the sole pilot and gunsman of a spaceship that was classed as Single-Use?

Find out online with Amazon or at www.sci-fi-author.com.

The blue touch paper is due to be lit in October 2020.

By the way...

In Come Again, Kalėdas means Christmas, in Lithuanian.

Bari means shepherd in Albanian. Pasti (in Russian) and Voskós (in Greek) also mean shepherd.

In Turkish, Koyun means sheep. Kutsal Isa is Holy Jesus. Bu Isa – It's Jesus. Kurtarici – The Saviour.

Door Ka Taara is Faraway Star in Hindi.

May the 4th be with us all

Printed in Great Britain
by Amazon